DRAGON ASSASSIN

A novel by

PIERS ANTHONY

J.R. RAIN

ISBN: 1500705039
ISBN 13: 9781500705039

ACCLAIM FOR J.R. RAIN
AND PIERS ANTHONY:

OTHER BOOKS BY PIERS ANTHONY AND J.R. RAIN

CHAPTER ONE

I t was another unproductive day.
I don't like unproductive days, especially as a self-employed private investigator living and working in the city of Los Angeles. Unproductive days meant I don't eat, pay my rent or pay my alimony. Hell, I hadn't had a haircut in months. I made it a new manly style, but the truth was I couldn't afford regular cuts. Unproductive days meant creditors would come knocking, and I hated when creditors came knocking.

Most important, unproductive days meant I didn't get to drink myself into oblivion, which is exactly what I'd been doing these past few months.

I was in my office, alone, my feet up on my old desk.

It wasn't much of an office—or a desk, for that matter. The office was just a small room with stained carpet, a couch on the far wall, where I had napped one too many times. The often-broken ceiling fan did little to disperse the hot air. A water cooler occasionally gurgled by a sink and faucet, where I kept my booze. An old TV sat on a bookshelf that was filled with novels I'd always meant to get to, but haven't found the time yet.

Not much of an office…and not much of a life, either. When I was working, I was usually tailing cheating wives, one or two of which I ended up cheating with myself.

Now, as the ceiling fan wobbled above, as the drone of traffic reached me from nearby Sunset Boulevard, I idly wondered how I could drum up more business. Perhaps start a Facebook account? Or even Twitter? Maybe both? Maybe now was a good time to see what, exactly, a Twitter was.

I hadn't a clue.

Truth was, I could barely use those new-fangled cell phones. You know, the ones that are practically a computer. Hell, I had a hard enough time with my laptop, let alone a computer the size of my palm.

I shook my head, and absently longed for the days when people actually used a land line. When a phone sounded like a phone, and not the latest Lady Gaga song.

I'd always suspected I was a man born out of time. As a kid, I often wore a cowboy hat and toy six-shooters to school—back when they allowed kids to bring toy guns to school. I longed to be a cowboy—hell, I still did. Now that was the life. No computers, no smart phones, no Twitter. Just me, my horse and the open range...

I awoke with a start.

How long I had been asleep, I didn't know. I'd been dreaming of the Wild West, of the Great Plains, of beautiful showgirls, and of whiskey. Mostly, I had dreamed briefly of long rides on my trusted horse, of its hooves pounding hard through the hot desert sand, kicking up dust a mile long behind me.

Oddly enough, as I sat up and rubbed my eyes, I was hearing just that: the sound of hooves.

"What the hell?" I mumbled.

I knew the sound of horse hooves well. Although I didn't have much, I always made a point of keeping a horse at a nearby stable, just outside of LA. Whenever I could, I took this horse out—and longed for simpler times.

The sound came again. Yes, hooves. In fact, many hooves.

"What the hell?" I said again, a little louder.

And just as I slid my cowboy boots off the desk and stood, I heard another strange sound: heavy boots approaching my office door. I'll admit, I briefly considered going for my gun located in the top right drawer, a gun I now kept nearby since an incident with a client's husband. Long story.

And so I stood there, undecided. I mean, was there really a horse just outside my door? Or had I imagined that? After all, wasn't I just dreaming of horses?

I nearly laughed. Of course, that was it.

I'd dreamed of the horses.

Maybe. I certainly wasn't dreaming of the approaching boots, which grew louder and louder. I considered again the gun in my drawer, and was just reaching for it when my office door opened.

All thoughts of my gun disappeared when I got a load of the man standing there in my office.

A man out of time, indeed.

———

The stranger was short, no more than an inch or two over five feet, and was wearing clothing that I was certain I'd never seen outside of the Renaissance fair. And even then, the clothes still seemed *off.* Just damn unusual. The man's shirt had a ruffled collar and wide stitching down the front. It appeared hand-stitched, and of a rough material that I was certain I'd never seen before.

Oh, and he wore a cape. Yes, a cape. As in Superman, minus the giant "S". It hung from his shoulder and nearly touched the ground and was embroidered with a material that looked, to my eye at least, like actual gold.

"What the hell?" I whispered yet again. Admittedly, my day had taken a dramatic turn to the weird.

Strangest of all, was the sword that hung from a scabbard at the man's right hip. Strange because it was an actual sword. A sword. Here in my office. And a highly unusual one at that. A bejeweled pommel poked up from the scabbard, a jewel unlike anything I'd ever seen before. Mostly because it seemed to be…

Glowing?

I shook my head. Surely, I was dreaming.

I was about to ask what the devil was going on when the stranger opened his mouth and...began to sing? And beautifully too...except he sang in a language I was certain I had never heard before.

And then it hit me—a singing telegram!

An old-fashioned special message. I nearly clapped, and was briefly relieved. After all, I'd been about to question my sanity. Yes, times have been rough of late. I was beginning to suspect too rough, that I'd finally lost it.

But, yes. A singing telegram.

And the guy sang beautifully...albeit in another language. Hungarian maybe?

I laughed and clapped and sat on the corner of my desk and enjoyed the show. One of my buddies had obviously set me up. Granted, I didn't have many buddies these days—and most were fellow private investigators. And, as I knew all too well, private investigators often had a *lot* of free time on their hands.

The man sang and sweated, and when he was done, I clapped again and offered him some water.

The little man frowned, scratched his head, then finally nodded. He next removed something from his pants pocket. It was a small pouch, held together with strips of colorful leather. The little man pulled open the pouch and proceeded to tap out something onto his open palm.

A white powder. Cocaine?

Next, the man did something highly unexpected. He raised his open palm to his face—and blew hard. The dust exploded out and quickly filled my small office.

"Hey," I said. "Why the hell did you do that?"

"I did it," said the man after a moment, "so that we might communicate. Can you understand me now?"

"Of course I can understand you," I muttered, coughing.

"The spell worked, I see. Very good. It's one of my own creations, in fact. The princess will be pleased."

"Spell? Princess?" I said, admittedly confused as hell. "Oh, I see, you're still in character. So, what are you, like a magician or something?"

"A wizard, in fact."

"Like Harry Potter and all that?"

"Harry Potter—" the man paused, cocked his head slightly. "Ah, you are referencing something in your popular culture. Yes, I suppose I am a little like Harry Potter and his gang of adventurers. There is, of course, one big difference."

"And what's that?"

"I'm a *real* wizard."

I grinned. "Of course you are."

"I see by your smile and easy agreement that you are using sarcasm. You are humoring me. You don't really believe me."

"I believe that you're quite a showman."

"In more ways than one, my good man."

"Now *that* I believe."

The man frowned slightly. It was almost as if he was, in fact, trying to understand me, or the intentions of my words. This day, certainly, could not have gotten any weirder.

He said, "Well, kind sir. My name is DubiGadlumthakathi— but you may call me Dubi—and I have no doubt that you will believe soon enough. You are Roan Quigley?"

I nodded, still grinning through all this madness.

He continued. "You are something called a private investigator?"

"Yes."

"And we are presently in the city of Los Angeles in the third dimensional physical realm of the planet Earth?"

I was about to grin again, but something suddenly stood out: the man sounded so…sincere. And so odd. I still could not place his accent. And had he really ridden up on an actual horse?

"Very good, then," said the man and reached inside another pocket. He extracted another pouch, this one clearly heavier than the first. I was certain I'd heard the clink of metal. And not just any metal. Gold? "We are here to hire you, Mr. Quigley."

I was momentarily caught off guard. "Hire me?"

"Of course. You do assist those in need, correct?"

"Yes, of course," I said, knowing that my grin was faltering a little.

"Well, Mr. Quigley, the Realm is very much in need of your expert services."

"The Realm?"

"Yes, Mr. Quigley. The Realm, from which we hail."

"Of course, right. And who's we?"

"Myself and the princess."

"Princess?"

"Yes, she's right outside your door. Would you care to meet her?"

"Er, I'm really quite busy—"

"I understand, which is why I've brought this."

And with that, the little man emptied onto his palm a dozen or so golden nuggets that looked, at least to my untrained eye, very real. Dubi said, "I trust this will be enough to retain your expert services?"

"Is that…?"

"Gold? Yes, Mr. Quigley, and there's more where that came from."

My mouth, inexplicably went dry, because I was certain—dead certain—that it was real gold. Real, honest-to-God gold. And tens of thousands of dollars worth of it.

"Sweet Jesus," I muttered.

"Your realm's deity, I assume?" asked Dubi.

"You assume correctly," I said, and did my best to get a handle on the situation. I sat back and crossed my arms over my chest. "So who set you up? Rick? My brother maybe?"

"Neither 'set me up,' or directed me to be here. I am here by the princess's directive only."

"Princess," I said. "Who's right outside the door?"

"Yes, with the others."

I stared at Dubi. He stared at me, smiling politely. I stared at the gold in his open palm. Then I pushed myself off the desk, and marched past the little man, who turned and followed me.

I stepped outside…and was not entirely prepared for what I saw…

———

The summer sun was high in the sky, baking the mostly empty parking lot. Mostly empty, since it was presently filled with six massive horses and four riders. Three men and one woman. Three heavily armed men, with broadswords that reached well below their boots. Even more weapons hung from various scabbards along the saddles.

They all regarded me curiously, especially the woman. I blinked in the bright light, trying my damnedest to comprehend what I was seeing, but I couldn't. For the life of me, I couldn't get a handle on what I was seeing: six horses, three warriors and a woman. Here in the middle of LA. On horseback.

And not just any woman, either. A stunning beauty who took my breath away—and who regarded me shyly.

I realized my mouth had dropped open, but I didn't care.

I was dreaming, of course. Or this was a seriously elaborate joke. Or I had lost my mind.

"I can see you're confused, my good man," said Dubi, coming up behind me. "I do not doubt that you are. Truth be known, this is a new experience for us all, too."

"What's going on?" I asked, still staring at the horses, at the weapons, at the stunningly beautiful woman sitting high above me.

"We're here to hire you, Mr. Quigley."

A very troubling thought suddenly occurred to me, one that made me doubt my sanity and to immediately swear off another drink: this is real.

"What, exactly, do you need me to do?" I heard myself ask.

"We need you to help us find a killer. An assassin, actually."

"An assassin?"

"Yes."

"And who did he assassinate?"

"The king, of course."

"Of course," I said. "The king. That makes perfect sense. And the young lady...?"

"Is his daughter."

I nodded, trying my damnedest to wrap my brain around what was happening to me...and couldn't.

"So why me?" I asked.

"We can explain that on the way," said the little man. "Really, we don't have much time to lose. The killer is getting away as we speak."

I felt dizzy. "I need to sit."

"We have provided you a horse, Mr. Quigley. We understand you are an expert rider."

"I...I feel sick."

"I am an expert at curing ailments, my good man. Please. We must hurry. We have a killer to catch. Will you help us?"

I looked at him, and looked at the horses—the beautiful horses. I longed to be astride such a beautiful creature. And then I looked at the princess. I sensed her sadness, her grief. Had her father actually been murdered? Assassinated?

And then she did something that warmed my heart and caused all doubt and confusion to melt away. She smiled at me.

"Yes," I said, barely able to believe the words that were coming from my mouth. "I will help you. I think."

"Very good!" said Dubi, clapping me on the shoulder and striding past me. "Then we must hurry. We haven't a moment to lose. Your mount awaits."

CHAPTER TWO

"Uh, one moment," I said. "I need something from the office."

"There is no time," Dubi protested. "We have food, clothing, swords, anything you'll need."

"This is special," I said, and dodged into the office before he could extend his protests. I went to the desk, grabbed my gun, a box of ammunition, and an underarm holster. I jammed them in place, then was about to head outside when I decided to grab my jacket, too, from the closet. After all, it might be hot here in LA; who knew what the weather was like in the Realm.

My steed was waiting by the door. At least the Wizard had had the sense to bring him up, and a fine horse he was. I mounted with dispatch and took the reins.

"Caution," Dubi warned. "That mount can be frisky with a strange rider."

I had already become aware of that. I nudged the stallion competently with my knees, letting him know that I knew what I was doing. A third party can't see the communication between a rider and his horse, but it is constantly there. He got the message and relaxed. I have a certain way with animals, especially horses. I respect them, but I take no guff from them. I could tell that this one was highly trained. We would get along.

We fell in in the middle, with two guards riding ahead, one behind, and wizard, princess, and me grouped in the middle. The horses knew their formation.

The posse set off at a swift trot. I noticed with surprise that now they trotted in step with each other, as they had not when they came. This was a really elite unit. But what would the good citizens of LA think of such a weird costumed group of mounted riders?

"I have cast an obscurity spell," Dubi said, answering my thought. "They don't notice us, or they see us as mechanical vehicles."

"Cars," I said.

"They are interesting," the princess said. "We have none in the Realm. They are more colorful than horses, but I think less personal."

"The Realm must be a fascinating place," I said, glancing at her, hoping to draw her out. I'm good at judging people; I have to be in my line of work. But the princess was largely a mystery as yet. She was riding lithely in the saddle, her bosom bouncing slightly, her hair flinging gently back. Perfection in motion!

"You are younger than we anticipated," the princess said. "The record indicated thirty years experience."

I laughed. "Your record is out of date. You are thinking of my father, who went by the same name. But he died last year under suspicious circumstances, and I took over."

"You have only one year experience?" Dubi asked, alarmed.

"Well, I did help Dad on occasion, learning the ropes from him. But yes, if you hired me for my thirty years in the trade, you'd better take your gold back, because I'm hardly the man Dad was."

Dubi made a face as if he was about ready to do that, but the princess cut in. "You lost your father!"

"As you lost yours," I agreed. "Hurts, doesn't it?"

"Oh, yes," she said, clouding up.

I hated that. "I'm sorry. I guess I was insensitive."

"No, it's that you understand."

"Oh, yes," I agreed, echoing her. Just like that, we had a bond.

"I don't have much experience governing, either," she said. "I was a protected child, especially after my mother was poisoned." The Realm evidently practiced hard-fisted politics. Now she had been rudely thrust into the cruel world of command. "My mother too. Breast cancer. I had to grow up in a hurry."

Dubi made another face, but didn't talk. I knew why: he had thought to hire a seasoned professional, and instead blundered into a novice with personal pains like those of the princess. He couldn't reverse course because he saw that the princess liked me, or at least liked my appreciation of her position. He was screwed.

The princess caught my eye. Tearfully, she smiled again. I returned the smile, my own vision blurring. What a pair we were!

"The access is in Griffin Park," Dubi said gruffly

"That's Griffith Park," I corrected him. "One of a number that enhance our fair city. It is known for its famous observatory and zoo."

He merely smiled obscurely. Then we came to the park, and I swear the sign said GRIFFIN PARK. It looked different, too. I was becoming more impressed with his magic.

We rode into the center. There was a kind of wavering in the air and ground, and I felt slightly ill, as I had before. Now I recognized it as a side effect of magic. As with sailing on a heaving ship, a landlubber gets motion sick at first. I was not accustomed to a magic environment.

The princess reached across and touched my arm. "The transition can feel awkward," she said. "I felt it when entering your Lost Angels realm. It will pass."

My queasiness fled at her touch. I don't know if that was medical, magical, or simply my thrill of contact with such a creature. "Thanks," I said. "It's passing already."

"Now you will meet my pet dragon," she said as we emerged to a phenomenal change of scenery. We were no longer in the city, but in an alien forest.

"Pet dragon?" I asked dumbly.

"Father gave her to me after my dear nanny died, to help protect me. She's warm."

Happiness was a warm dragon, I thought. "Okay." It seemed ironic that the dragon had not been on hand to protect the king from assassination. But there was surely more to this situation than met the (private) eye. Dragons, I was sure, were not the cuddly pets normally given to children.

And there it was, blocking the path ahead. Think of a twelve foot long (snout to tail) alligator with wings, fiery breath, and attitude.

The horses halted, unbidden. They clearly were not afraid of the dragon, probably because it was a member of the party, but they respected it.

"You must meet her yourself, alone, the first time," the princess said. "So that she knows you, as she knows Dubi and the horses. Do not be concerned; she knows you are joining the party."

Like a guard dog sniffing the hand of a new person, I thought, zeroing him in as someone to be tolerated. I could handle that.

I dismounted and walked to meet the dragon. Her copious lip curled in an expression of contempt as she saw me. Oh, yeah? I thought, my own lip curling. As I mentioned, I don't take guff from animals.

I stood before her. Her eyes were on the sides of her head, but able to focus forward. Our gazes met.

The dragon faded, to be replaced by a six foot tall warrior woman, a virtual Amazon wearing scale armor. "Hurt my mistress and I will hurt you," she said.

Now this was really interesting! The animal was telepathic, and could project an illusion image that could talk. That was a nice device for communication. However, as a friendly introduction it lacked somewhat.

I'm normally a reasonably easygoing guy, not looking for trouble. But I get riled when threatened. So I reacted a bit sharply.

I kept my mouth shut and responded mentally, so that only the dragon could hear me. "Do you know what a gun is, bitch?"

"No. Is it like the elastic candy my mistress chews?"

Chewy candy? Then I got it: she heard gun as gum. "No. It's a weapon. Trust me, hothead, you don't want to encounter it."

She was unfazed. "Can it strike beyond flame range?"

I made a quick calculation of the likely range of a jet of flame: maybe her body length. "Oh, yes."

She considered. She had to know from our mental contact that I was not bluffing and not afraid. I had a weapon to match hers, and knew how to use it. That had to be respected. I remembered another saying, that an armed society was a polite society. This interchange would pass for politeness. "We'll get along," she decided.

"Not so fast, tailpipe. We're both on the same side. We have two ways to do this. We can tolerate each other, staying clear when possible. Or we can work together for the benefit of the princess, who is not my mistress."

She caught the mental nuance. She laughed, with smoke coming out of her mouth, nose, and ears. That was nice imagery. "Not yet."

Along about that point I began to like her. "We'll get along," I agreed. "What's your name?"

"I am called Fiera, to my friends."

"And I am Roan, to my friends."

"I greet you, Roan."

"I greet you, Fiera."

Then the Amazon dissipated and the flying alligator was back. But we had our understanding, and the mental rapport was maintained. I could now talk to Fiera anytime, mentally. That was likely to be useful when things got tough, as they were likely to when dealing with the assassin. I turned about and returned to my mount, while the dragon spread her huge wings and took off into the sky.

"Now she knows you," the princess said as the march resumed. "She won't scorch you."

"We came to an understanding," I agreed. "We respect each other, and I like her."

"You talked to her!" she said, surprised.

"To Fiera," I agreed. "I thought that was the point of our meeting."

She lowered her voice confidentially. "Please, only Dubi and I know. Don't tell."

That the dragon was intelligent and telepathic? I gathered that not all dragons were that way. Fiera was special, and probably ten times as effective as a guardian because of it. "My lips are sealed," I agreed.

Now it was time to get down to business. "I gather you are on the trail of the assassin—the man who assassinated your father the king," I said. "I am trained to search out clues, but this magic realm is not my usual bailiwick. Can you give me some more information?"

"I will do that, in due course," Dubi said. "We can spare the princess the ugly details."

"That's fine," I agreed. At the moment I didn't see how my gumshoe expertise could help trace a criminal who used magic. But I really wanted to help the princess if I could.

CHAPTER THREE

W e rode on.
The Realm was everything I had ever dreamed of as a boy and, admittedly, as an adult, too. Far blue mountains, mist-shrouded forests, trails that could lead, quite possibly, to anywhere. All enjoyed while riding high on a horse, and with a beautiful companion.

Granted, that beautiful companion had a few companions of her own: three warriors and a wizard. Yes, not exactly how I dreamed it, but who was complaining?

I was far away from the drudgery of my simple life, of dealing with my often-angry ex-wife, and of following yet another cheating spouse.

I hated following cheating spouses.

Fiera scouted above us, often flying many hundreds of feet ahead, and then circling back. On one such occasion, I tested the limits of my new-found telepathy with the creature.

Can you hear me, Fiera? Now that she was no longer generating the Amazon image, it was straight thought, not a seeming voice.

Of course, Roan.

How far must you be before you cannot hear me?

Fifty clacks.

What's fifty clacks?

I heard a deep chuckling inside my head, an odd experience at best. *Very far, Roan.*

Once or twice the princess looked back at me, only to smile shyly and then look forward again. I smiled, too, but often too late. Her glances were only fleeting at best. The princess was an expert rider, and her hips, I noted, moved well with the motion of the horse.

My divorce had been nasty—and scarring. I hadn't dated or wanted to date since that travesty. Instead, I had thrown myself into building a budding agency, following in my father's footsteps, applying everything he'd learned.

Unfortunately, my father was from the old guard. His business had been built on good work, good relationships and good people. He hadn't had to deal with the proliferation of internet web sites that did a lot of my work for me. He never had to advertise on Google or Facebook. He never had to figure out what a Twitter was. All of which seemed necessary to make it in today's world.

Not this world, I thought.

Excuse me, Roan? asked the flying dragon, glancing over its scaly shoulder. It was, perhaps, a few hundred feet before us. Or maybe a clack or two, whatever the hell those were.

Er, sorry, I thought. That was intended for me.

Then you need to learn how to shield your thoughts, human. I am not the only entity who can read thoughts. Indeed, there are many who can, and some who are not as nice as me.

Shielding thoughts is possible?

Of course.

And she proceeded to tell me how, a process that involved creating a sort of mental wall around myself, a wall that was created by intention.

Intention?

Indeed, Roan. *Intention is always the first step to reality.*

Perhaps in this world, I thought. *In my world, the first step to making anything a reality is hard work.*

I prefer our world, my new friend. Yours sounds like too much work.

Nothing wrong with too much work.

Perhaps not, Roan. *Then again, you might think a little differently after some time in our own.*

I tested shielding my thoughts, and it seemed to work. I called out once or twice to the flying dragon and was subsequently ignored. Unless, of course, the flying beast had tricked me into thinking my thoughts had been shielded.

All of which, of course, was giving me a big headache.

We continued on as a light rain began to fall. There wasn't much in the way of animals along the wide trail. Once or twice I saw something large and hairy dart through the forest, but the horses didn't seem alarmed, and so I wasn't either. I kept my weapon concealed under my jacket. I didn't know much about magical realms, but I figured if Dubi's magic worked in our world, then my gun should work here.

The rain increased. The princess, whose name I had not yet been given, pulled up her hood. I noted the massive ring on her right hand. Did such a ring imply marriage? Or that she was of royalty? Or, perhaps, had a penchant for nice things?

Fiera, I thought, lowering my mental wall. *Can I ask you a question about the princess?*

The dragon was now only a mere dot in the sky. Certainly many clacks from me now.

You can ask me any question you like, human. Whether I answer is something else.

Fair enough. Is the princess married?

You mean, does she have a life mate?

Yes. A life mate.

There was a slight pause before the dragon's voice filled my thoughts: *There is one who seeks her hand in such a union.*

Ah, I thought, more disappointed than I thought I would be. *So she is taken?*

I did not say taken, human. She is being pursued. The union could prove beneficial to the realm.

Then why not get married? I asked.

From what I understand about my mistress, although I do not pry very deeply into her personal life, is that she does not love her pursuer.

Love is important to her? I asked.

17

Very much, Roan. And I can sense your excitement. My advice is to let it go. The princess can only enter into a union with royalty. It is written.

I see, I thought, and once again shielded my thoughts.

We were now on a dark forest trail, with interlocking branches forming a sort of tunnel around us. True, we were shielded from the rain, but not the bigger drops of water. The warriors seemed to be tense in here. In fact, I even saw one of them unconsciously reach for his weapon.

Dubi pulled on his reins and slipped back to me, riding by my side.

"The road to the kingdom is fraught with challenges, Detective Roan."

"You can just call me Roan."

"So be it."

"What kind of challenges?" I asked.

"Of the human kind, bandits."

I didn't like where this was going. "And of the inhuman kind?"

"Orcs."

"What, exactly, is an orc?"

"Blood-thirsty beasts. Humanoid but not human. They thrive on death and destruction. Not very pleasant creatures."

I shifted my gun handle a little, for easier access. The orcs didn't sound pleasant at all. I sat a little straighter in my saddle, and scanned the surroundings.

"Don't fear, Roan," said Dubi. "The horses will alert us first to the orcs. It's the bandits we have to fear most."

I nodded and decided that the kingdom was suddenly decidedly less enchanting than I had first thought. You take the good with the bad, I supposed.

"Why do you need my help, Dubi? I'm not even of your world."

"It was seen that you would help us, Roan."

"Seen by who?"

He glanced at me. "By me."

"Except you actually saw my father, and ended up with me."

"Perhaps."

"Trust me, I'm not even half as good as my father…" I trailed off. It was still hard talking about my father.

"Perhaps we are not looking for a good man," said Roan.

"I don't understand."

"Perhaps we are looking for the right man."

I frowned, puzzling through his words, realizing that I might very well be in way over my head—and wondering just how I might get back home. I hadn't thought about that. I had been so eager to get away, that I never stopped to think how I might get back.

I was just about to ask that very question, when something that looked remarkably like an arrow shaft suddenly appeared in the back of the guard directly in front of the princess.

"Bandits!" someone shouted.

CHAPTER FOUR

The wounded guard fell off his horse, obviously dead. The two remaining guards whirled on their steeds, drawing their swords and they lifted their small shields. Dubi's horse lurched closer to mine. "Stay close," he snapped. "I have a shield."

Indeed, more arrows were already flying, and veering off as they were about to strike us. It was as though there were an invisible metal cone around us that deflected the shafts. Unfortunately the bandits were also invisible, effectively hidden in the foliage. How many arrows could the shield stop? We were sitting ducks.

"The princess!" I said. For she was sitting on her horse, a little apart, making no effort to hide or escape.

"She has her own shield," Dubi said. "Anyway, they won't try to kill her."

"Why not?" I asked as my eyes scanned the network of foliage around us, trying to spot the attacking bandits.

"She's worth more in ransom than all the rest of us together. They mean to kill us and take her."

Now I had the picture. "I need to get out of your shield."

"You may be ignorant, but you're not crazy. Stay put."

"If the shield stops arrows, it may also stop bullets. I can't shoot through it."

"If a bullet is like an arrow, that is true. However you are safe here. Let the guards handle it. They are competent."

"One's already dead. I have to help."

"Do not risk yourself unnecessarily."

But I was already dismounting and forging forward, escaping the shield as I drew my gun. *Fiera!*

I can't get there in time. The branches balk me from reaching you, and I could not fly in that restricted place anyway. It is a cunning ambush.

Yes, the bandits had chosen well, to nullify the princess' primary defense. They must have shielded their thoughts so the dragon was not alerted to their presence as we approached. But my siege mentality was already operating. *Strafe the foliage from above. Set it on fire.*

She was dubious. *This will not halt the attack.*

Don't debate it! I snapped. *Do it!*

I felt her circling, orienting. Then I saw fire in the treetops, blasting down between the branches, scorching the leaves, setting the twigs afire. The tunnel of our path was becoming a tube of flames. *Good. Now land ahead and come back here afoot.*

She did not argue, perceiving what was in my mind. Meanwhile the fire spread.

"Yow!" a man cried as he got burned.

That identified his location. I shot him. He groaned and dropped to the ground, not knowing what else had hit him.

"Hey!" I fired at that sound too, and he groaned and fell. *How many are there?* I asked Fiera.

Six.

So there were four to go. I saw a figure move, avoiding the flame, and shot him too. Three down.

Now the guards, a bit slow on the uptake, advanced on the flames, swords ready.

I am impressed with your gun, Fiera thought.

Job's not finished. I scanned the flames for the others.

A guard returned to stand beside me. He thought it was all over?

Something flashed from a low tangle. I realized that it was another bandit, this one with a crossbow, so I hadn't seen any motion of drawing an arrow. I whirled to plug him, and knew I got him, but the bolt was already on the way. It was too late even to duck.

The guard beside me extended the flat of his sword in a lightning motion. The bolt smacked into it, emitting a cracking sound and a spark before dropping to the ground. Right in front of my face.

I stared at the fallen bolt, then at the guard. He had acted with precision, the moment it was required, intercepting the bolt in mid air. He had known exactly what he was doing.

"You boys didn't even need my help," I said. "Reflexes like that—"

He merely turned away.

The last two bandits are fleeing. They have seen your weapon in action. The numbers are no longer in their favor.

Oh, shit! *Can you point me to a bandit?*

Why? We have won this engagement. There is no longer danger from them.

Just do it, please.

Then through the brush and diminishing flames I saw a figure, hunching down, running clumsily away. *Thanks!* I launched myself into pursuit.

I think the bandit might have outrun me, but it never occurred to him that I would be reversing the attack. By the time he saw me I was close enough to tackle him. I brought him down hard, then wrestled one of his arms behind in a hammerlock. "Stop struggling," I told him.

Realizing that I had the advantage, not to mention the pain hold, he obeyed. I let him go and stepped back, holding the gun on him. "Make my day," I said.

He might not know the reference, but he was pretty sure I could hurt him if he gave me reason. Certainly the two guards could. He stood up, facing me, silent.

Dubi and the princess came up. "Kill him," Dubi said. "He's dangerous. He will strike the moment he gets the chance."

"Not yet," I said. "I'm waiting for the dragon."

Fiera was already approaching. *Kill him. He's a treacherous knave.*

I spoke to the bandit. "What's your name?"

He paused briefly, then answered. "Boffo."

True. But that's about all he'll tell you.

"Boffo, I need to know who sent you here, and why."

He gazed at me with something like a sneer hovering in the vicinity of his ugly face. He was concluding that I was an ignoramus who could be fooled. "You're obviously wealthy travelers with gold to steal and a pretty wench to rape. So we went after you. It's what we do for a living."

He's lying.

"Now Boffo, there are two ways we can do this," I said seriously. "You can answer my questions as fully and honestly as possible, and I will let you go unharmed. Or you can be balky, or try to lie to me, and I will have the dragon roast you alive. It will take you a while to die in utter agony with your skin fried; you wouldn't like it. You have three chances. You have used up one. I ask you again: who sent you, and why?"

"I already answered you, idiot!"

"That's two." I glanced at the dragon, who obligingly puffed out a little cloud of smoke. "Final time: who?"

Now the bandit realized that he was done. "We were ordered to intercept you here. To kill the men and take the princess captive, for ransom."

True.

"That's better. *Who* ordered you?"

"I don't know," he said, alarmed. "I swear! I'm just a lowly bandit; our leader got the order. He's gone."

True.

I considered. So I had gotten the wrong man. It had hardly been worth it. All I had done was confirm what we pretty well knew already: they were after the princess.

I sighed. "Okay. I gave my word. Take off."

But Boffo just stood there. "I can't."

This was curious. "Why not?"

"Because now I've squealed, I'll be marked for death. You might as well kill me. Only not by burning alive. Make it fast and clean."

True.

I sighed again. That would teach me to give my word ignorantly. Well, I would have to work it out. "We now have a spare horse. We'll take you to where you aren't known, and let you go there. Will that do?"

He eyed me cannily. "Sure. But they'll track me down regardless."

I thought fast. "Okay. We'll garb you like the dead guard, and you'll take his place. We'll put your clothes on his body and scorch it so it's unrecognizable. Then they'll figure you're dead and won't look for you. You'll be free and safe as long as you stay well clear of your former associates."

Boffo nodded. "That might work."

He takes you for a fool for keeping your word. He'll back-stab you when he has the chance and make a run for it. He's a complete rogue; he can't be trusted.

Damn. Why had I ever messed in with this business? I just kept getting in deeper.

The princess stepped forward. "I will handle it."

I was surprised. "You will handle this rogue? How?"

"I will kiss him. Then he will behave."

"You can't trust him!" I protested. "He'd as soon rape you as look at you!"

"You got that right, rube," Boffo muttered. "She's a looker."

The princess went to the bandit. She took his head between her hands, held it in place, and kissed him on the lips. I simply stared, appalled by her naivete.

Then Boffo dropped to his knees. "Lady!" he cried. "I worship you! Command me."

"Just do as Sir Roan says." She turned away from him. "He is now my love slave," she told me. "He will not harm me or betray me in any way. The effect will last about three days. That should be time enough."

True.

"I'll be dipped in spit," I breathed. I had just learned something astonishing about the princess. She was not at all defenseless. In fact, no member of this party was any pushover. Then it hit me: *Sir* Roan?

She gave you a title to facilitate your work. That is her prerogative.

Oh. We made the exchange, while the princess discreetly faced away, laying the dead guard in the path in the bandit's clothes and scorching him enough. The others we left where they had fallen. The surviving bandits would discover them in due course and perhaps take warning.

"We shall have to notify the guard's kin that he died honorably," I said. "But that we could not recover his body."

"It shall be done," Dubi said. "These men are accustomed to hardship and death. His kin will be well taken care of."

"They shall be," the princess agreed.

Boffo was now in the guard's clothing and armor, girt with his weapons. It was a reasonable fit, considering he was not as large or muscular as the guard. "I had hoped to take this outfit as booty," he said. "Now I don't care, as long as I can serve the princess."

Then we all mounted and resumed our trek. "I think we found the right man," Dubi said.

"No way! I fouled everything up and had to be bailed out by the princess."

"You did not lose your wits in a crisis," he said. "You acted with dispatch, organizing an effective counterattack. You used your weapon to excellent effect. You obtained necessary information. You worked out a feasible continuation when there was a problem. This is the kind of assistance we require. Neither the princess nor I are good organizers or fighters. You will do."

"I just did what I had to do. If I'd had more time, I would have figured out something better. As it was, it was ragged." And I had needed to be saved by a guard.

"Cease debating, or the princess will kiss you."

I glanced at the princess, and she met my gaze and smiled faintly. She didn't need to kiss me to wipe out my individual volition; she was well on the way to doing that already. I shut up.

I realized that when Fiera had teased me about the princess becoming my mistress, she had meant it in the same way as Boffo. My absolute ruler. She had literal magic.

True.

And what other significant things did I have to learn about the Realm? I feared I was in way over my head. Yet such was the inherent magic of the situation, I did not mind. Much of what I had daydreamed about before, was actually coming to pass, in its weird fashion.

I noticed that Boffo, riding in the guard's place just ahead of us, was scowling. I moved up to talk to him. "You look angry. What's the problem? Haven't I treated you fairly?"

"I don't have to talk to you, pisshead!" he said gruffly. I was intrigued by the way the language translation spell handled insults. "We made a deal. That's all."

"A deal in the interest of protecting the princess," I reminded him. "I'm still learning about this Realm."

"I love her, not you."

He was starting to get to me. "I am working for her. She would be dismayed if you balked my helping her."

He was rebelliously silent. I glanced back to catch the eye of the princess. She cleared her throat loud enough to be heard.

Boffo melted. "What do you want? I've told you what little I know."

"I want to know why you were scowling."

"That's relevant?"

"It could be."

"It's not you," he said. "I am not your friend. You're a foreign simpleton, but you kept your word. I'm not mad at you."

So he was being honest. "Who, then?"

"At the traitor who gave us the assignment. We were set up."

"*You* were set up?"

"Sent to ambush a party with masked Class A Warriors. Might as well ambush a dragon with a toothpick. We weren't supposed to succeed. We got wiped out just to make a stupid point. We'd never have taken the mission if we had known."

This is interesting. I am reading his thoughts as they come to the surface.

I found it interesting too, remembering the almost casual way the guard had saved my life. Those were inhuman reflexes. A Class A Warrior? I had sudden respect. The bandit didn't even know about the mental powers of the dragon, and I was not about to tell him. This was a truly high-powered party. "Why, then?"

"That's what I'm figuring out now. The only thing I can think of is as a warning to the princess: she faces real danger if she persists in trying to be independent."

"And what about me?"

"What *about* you? Why did they make a risky trip to pick up a doofus like you? They certainly didn't need you to defend them, even with your deadly alien weapon. There's something else going on."

Exactly my conclusion. Too bad it had required a scoundrel bandit to reason out the obvious. I suspected it would be pointless to ask either Dubi or the princess. Especially if I, too, were being set up in some way.

Those guards had been slow to react, letting me take the lead. Why? Because they were under orders to let me do my stuff, as long as I didn't hurt myself. So I had performed, like a seal at a water show, and it seemed Dubi and the princess were satisfied. Did they really need a foreign private eye? That seemed unlikely. But that left the mystery of why they had gone to the trouble of fetching me from L.A., and why the princess was being nice to me.

Are you in on this, Fiera?

No. I share your confusion. They clearly need you for something, but not for what we thought.

27

That was vaguely reassuring. The others might have secrets, but the dragon was being straight with me.

True.

"You're catching on," Boffo said. "You're another patsy, like me."

"I wouldn't say that."

"No? At least I know my love for the princess is magic, and will wear off. The irony is that I don't even want it to; I want to grovel at her hem forever. But she didn't kiss *you*. What's your excuse?"

"You asshole!" I muttered.

He merely looked knowingly at me.

I left him and fell back to rejoin the princess, saying nothing about anything. What would be the point?

CHAPTER FIVE

We continued on.
Admittedly, I wasn't sure what the hell was going on. In fact, I wasn't even entirely sure I hadn't completely lost my mind back there in my office in Los Angeles. Maybe I had. But if riding high upon a powerful horse, with a telepathic dragon flying above and a beautiful princess before me meant that I was going crazy...well, sign me up.

If this is crazy, I don't want to be sane.

True, I may not know what the hell was going on, and, yes, I might currently be babbling incoherently in some insane asylum, but the one thing I was sure of was this: I had been hired to do a job. I had been hired to track down a killer. An assassin.

Insane or not, I was damn well going to finish the job—and collect that pouch of gold, too.

As I was idly wondering just how I would actually deposit a pouch of gold over at my bank, the forest trail opened onto a grassy meadow and, in the far distance, I could see an actual castle.

We soon came upon all manner of dwellings, from small thatched homes, to bigger stone structures. All who saw us bowed deeply, many smiling at the princess. I noted the guards closed ranks around her, although she didn't notice. She smiled back and even waved.

So she was a kind ruler, well-loved by those in the Realm. Although I was not surprised, this greatly relieved me. I would have questioned my judgment had I discovered I was smitten by someone cruel and reviled. And the one thing an investigator can never do is question his judgment or assessment of people. Sometimes that was the only thing we had.

The grassy meadow soon turned into a cobblestone road and now we were in a bustling village. Everywhere we went, people bowed and smiled, but if they got too close the guards gently pushed them aside.

Fiera, I noted, had briefly disappeared.

Where are you? I asked the dragon.

Nearby. The villagers tend to panic when they see me or my shadow.

But you are a good dragon.

Not always. I'm a protective dragon, which means I will burn you to a crisp, too, if I think you are a threat to my mistress.

Understood, I thought, and shivered a little.

Few looked at me or the ruffian, although I did garner a stare or two. As we entered the open market, which was filled stalls selling everything from meats to weapons to clothing, I noticed one man in particular watching me.

Every good investigator is alert for a tail, and this guy was definitely tailing us. We'd picked him up at the entrance into the village, where I'd first spotted him lounging against a bale of hay.

Now, he was plodding along on an old nag of a horse, and keeping pace at a safe distance. Maybe I shouldn't be too surprised. Perhaps the princess making an appearance in the village was a rarity. Maybe it was common for people to follow along.

No, not necessarily. Most smiled and waved at their princess, while she smiled and nodded back—and then returned to their work.

I kept my eye on him—a short man with a long, blond beard—but never so long that I gave away that I knew we were being followed. As far as I was aware, none of the guards had noticed him, and Dubi seemed to almost be asleep in the saddle.

We came upon a stall selling freshly-baked breads, and the princess held up her hand, and her two remaining guards—and one faithful—if briefly enchanted—scoundrel, instantly stopped.

As the princess slid out of her saddle to survey the breads, I tugged on Dubi's robe. "I'll be back," I said.

The wizard snorted and nearly fell out of his saddle. Son-of-a-bitch, he *had* been asleep. "Where are you going, Roan?"

"Business," I said, kicking my heels and pulling on the reins.

"What kind of business?"

"The kind you hired me for," I said, and shot through an opening between the stalls, scattering something that might have been chickens but looked like winged furry balls.

Once out of the busy market and behind the milling crowds, I saw the bearded man. He'd been keeping pace with us. But now he saw me, too, charging at him. His mouth dropped comically—and he heeled his mount, slapping its flank, but the old nag barely got faster than a light trot. He quickly gave up and leaped from his saddle, rolling twice, and found his feet. He stumbled and dashed off through the high grass.

I bore down on him. My own mount was a true war horse. Massive, powerful, fast. And, above else, fearless. It charged through the high grass. It snorted and almost seemed to take delight in the chase.

Of course, human, came a deeper thought. This wasn't Fiera. *I love nothing more than to engage in battle.*

Who said that?

Who do you think?

I tore my gaze off the fleeing little man. Had the horse spoken telepathically to me?

Would be the more likely answer, would it not?

The fleeing man looked over his shoulder, tripped, rolled once or twice and was back on his feet. We were getting ever closer. In fact, the horse even seemed to pick up speed.

Of course, I'm picking up speed. We're going to lose him.

I saw what the horse meant. The little man was making a mad dash for a row of buildings.

Hurry!

My pleasure, human.

And the horse hit another gear, pounding faster through the grass than I had ever ridden before. Yes, a war horse indeed!

Still, as fast as we covered the ground, the little man was just too far ahead. He hung a sharp right and darted between two buildings. The horse slowed on its own volition, and I dismounted, too, stumbling but not falling. Soon, I was dashing down the same narrow alley—and quickly found myself on another bustling street. A very different kind of street. Cops would have called this the red light district. Women of questionable morals loitered on street corners. Taverns everywhere. Two men fighting across the street. One man vomiting just to my right. Nowhere to be seen was the little, bearded man who had been following us. I frowned, frustrated, then headed back to the horse.

Can all animals read thoughts? I asked the horse.

I do not know, human. I'm only a horse.

Another voice appeared in my thoughts. It was Fiera. *His answer is a valid one, Sir Roan. As I scan his thoughts I can see he has never connected to another human.*

I see, I thought. *I think. Is it common for horses to connect with their riders?*

As far as I'm aware, no, came the dragon's reply.

Then why me? I asked.

I think it would be best to have the Magician Dubi answer your question.

Am I going crazy, Fiera? I suddenly asked.

You appear to be of sound mind, Sir Roan.

Which is exactly what a hallucination would tell a deranged mind.

Fiera chuckled. *Be easy on yourself, human.*

Fine, I thought. *Who was the man following us?*

I did not have time to orientate on his mind, but I did catch that he was reporting to someone on our travels.

Any idea who?

Sadly, no.

I frowned and headed back to the market, where the princess was just wrapping up her purchases. She seemed unaware that

I had been gone. Dubi scanned me quickly, and I wondered if he, too, could read my thoughts. Once we continued on, the magician rode up next to me. "You have made contact with your mount, I see."

"Er, yes. Is that a problem?"

"Not a problem at all. But very interesting."

"Interesting, why?"

Dubi didn't immediately answer; in fact, he seemed to be debating something. We left the market behind us, and soon found ourselves on a cobbled path that led, I suspected, to the castle high above. After a few minutes, Dubi answered, "Only royal blood have such connections."

I laughed. "Royal blood? You're saying I'm of royal blood?"

"Trust me, I'm as confused as you are."

"But aren't you like a master magician? Don't you know everything?"

Now Dubi laughed. "Hardly, Sir Roan. I am only the royal family's personal magician."

"Kind of like Merlin," I said.

"Merlin, yes. A good friend of mine, but that's another story. But, yes, I act in a similar capacity, giving counsel to the royal family as they see fit, and sometimes..."

"Sometimes as *you* see fit," I finished.

"Well, yes. They trust my judgment."

"Why am I really here, Dubi? Your Class A guards are surely competent enough to sniff-out the assassin. Why drag me here all the way from my world?"

Dubi's blue eyes sparkled. "If I recall, Sir Roan, you came willing enough."

"Well, yes. In some ways, your appearance answered a call within me."

"A call for what, my friend?"

"For something more in life, something different. Something magical. Something adventurous. I have dreamed of quests all my life."

The magician nodded. "In a way, we have heard your call, I suspect. In a way, I think your yearning was in response to us here in the Realm."

"What do you mean?"

"You were meant to be here, Sir Roan."

"I don't understand."

Roan reached out and placed a warm hand on my forearm. "You inherited your love of horses from your father, true?"

"Yes. He was an avid rider."

"Did your father ever speak much of his past?"

I thought about that. "No, not always. He was an orphan without a past. He didn't know his parents."

Dubi's eyes softened, and I caught the meaning behind him. "No…" I began, knowing my mouth had dropped open.

"Yes, my friend."

"My father…"

"Your father was in grave danger, and so the decision was made to keep him safe." He held my gaze. "He was taken to your world."

"But…why?"

"It is a long story—"

"Then cut it short," I snapped, then softened my tone. "Please. I need to know. I'm kind of freaking out here."

"The king had an affair with a woman who gave birth to a son…" he let his voice trail off.

"My father," I said, my voice so faint I almost couldn't hear it.

"Indeed. He was safe for a time."

I grabbed Dubi's wrist, the gesture was enough to nearly pull the old wizard from his saddle. "My father was killed, Dubi. Under, I believe, suspicions circumstances."

The wizard didn't struggle. Instead, he looked at me sadly. "Not suspicious, my friend. Your father was murdered, as well."

Something tore through me. Pain and anger. "I…" I struggled for words but couldn't find them.

Dubi laid a gentle palm on my hand. "Someone is systematically assassinating royal blood. You were going to be next. And so was…"

I looked at the princess, my mouth dropping again.

"Yes," answered the magician. "The princess, too."

My spinning brain did the genealogical calculations. "That would make the princess my father's half sister...my aunt."

"In theory. But she is not of royal blood."

"I don't understand."

"The king was a very old man when he was assassinated, my friend. The princess came to him late in life."

"Came to him? She is adopted?"

"Yes."

I thought I might get dizzy. Although I was still holding tightly onto the wizard's wrist, I was fairly certain it was he who was keeping me from losing my balance upon the mount.

"A lot to comprehend at one time, I know, my friend," he said gently. "But better now than later."

I nodded, and released his arm. My father had been murdered. The princess was adopted. My father was of royal blood. I was of royal blood. Someone was systematically assassinating the royal family. I was next, and so was the princess.

Yes, a lot to comprehend. Perhaps even too much. I thought of my father. We hadn't been close these past two years. I had always thought he and I would rekindle our relationship. His premature death removed that option.

Not death, I thought. *His murder.*

"And you do not know who killed my father or my..."

"Your grandfather? No, I do not. The assassin is unknown to me."

"So you need my help after all."

"Indeed."

I set my jaw and leaned forward a little in the saddle. "I want you to show me where my grandfather was killed." I didn't know much, but I knew how to solve a crime.

"Very well, Sir Roan," said the old wizard, nodding, and we continued up to the castle.

CHAPTER SIX

Then I got an idea. I rode over to join Boffo. "That spy I chased—did you recognize him?"

"You figure one criminal should know another?" he inquired caustically.

"I figure he might. That man was obviously spying on the princess."

"Oh, unicorn turds!" he swore. He didn't like me, but he had to help the princess. "Yes. He's a low-level skulker who does work for Lord Mephisto."

Bulls-eye! "And why would Lord Mephisto be tracking the princess?"

"He's a rival claimant to the throne. Distant lineage, no chance unless all royals are gone." Then he did a double-take. "That's why we were sent after the princess. Not for hostage, but for Mephisto to marry, so he could claim the throne. If by some freak mischance we killed the Warriors and actually captured her."

"You don't approve?"

"It'd have been fine with me. Until she kissed me. Now I want to cut his balls off and stuff them up his rump before I start torturing him."

What a difference love made! "Thank you," I said unnecessarily, and rejoined Dubi. "That spy I chased—he works for Lord Mephisto."

"Who is number one on my suspicion list," Dubi said darkly. "But we can't prove it."

36

And couldn't risk an accusation without solid evidence. Ever thus. They did need my services.

We came to the castle. It was a fine fortress in itself, with a moat formed by a divided river, massive outer walls, and lofty turrets. The drawbridge cranked down and clanked into place so we could ride across. I saw crossbows lining the crenelated wall immediately ahead; no unwanted intruders would pass.

But once we passed the exterior battlements, the castle was surprisingly gracious. Tapestries were hung on the walls, and ornamental plants decorated the courtyard where we dismounted. Grooms came to take the horses.

"We will rejoin you soon, princess," Dubi said. Then he led me down a side hall, through winding passages, and up a spiral staircase to a crowded chamber about five stories up. It was lined with books and dolls.

"I am not making much sense of this," I said.

"The king and his last mistress shared this suite, before she died," Dubi explained. "It reflects their tastes."

"That mistress—would that be the nanny who took care of the princess?"

"The same. The king and his daughter both adored her."

Albeit for different reasons, I thought. "She evidently liked dolls."

"So it was mooted. Actually the dolls were his, the books hers."

"He played with dolls?"

"Not exactly. Royals tend to have magic. These are what you would call doovoo dolls."

"Voodoo," I said.

"Voodoo," he agreed getting it right. "Every key person in the kingdom was represented here by his or her doll. When they did not properly honor the rules of the kingdom, he could make them uncomfortable. They soon fell in line."

"I can imagine," I said. Voodoo dolls were said to transmit whatever they experienced to the people they emulated. Heat a doll's feet, and the relevant person would find himself walking on coals, though none showed. There would be nothing he could directly do about it.

I considered the dolls with new interest. Surely one was Lord Mephisto. Some were rather pretty females. "What of these?"

"When the king got a hankering for the close company of a comely young lady, he would start removing her doll's clothing and stroking its body. She would soon get the message, and report for bed duty."

"And if she was not inclined?"

"She might be annoyed, but she would obey. The dolls can kill, if handled roughly enough. No woman was ever disinclined to the king's face."

"But some might be angry enough to kill," I said.

"Unlikely. It was an honor to be favored by the king, so most were quite willing, and the others accepted it as the price of an excellent castle employment."

No real motive there, then. "Yet someone killed him."

"Yes. Here is the site." He showed me out to a balcony. Here the chill wind swept smartly by, and the ground was far below. The wizard did not venture out onto the balcony, pointing instead. "He was out here when an arrow appeared, killing him instantly."

"But the ground is far away," I protested. "How could an archer loose an arrow across the moat and to a target this high, to this effect?" Then I paused. "Could a Class A Warrior have done it?"

"Yes, with difficulty. It would be a lucky shot, considering the ramparts and the wind, especially at night. But none would. All Warriors are totally loyal."

So they believed. "The arrow," I said. "Naturally you examined it. Especially for some kind of magic assist."

"Naturally," he agreed. "It was a standard issue type, effectively anonymous. There was undefined magic associated with it, perhaps to guide it, possibly to lend it extra power. Nothing I could identify with any certainty."

"Could the assassin have been closer?" I asked. "Riding a dragon or something?"

Dubi choked. "Dragons are not steeds! They haul meat into the air only to carry it to their nests for more leisurely devouring. In any event, their flight is uneven. It would be extremely difficult to make an accurate shot."

True, Fiera's thought came. I didn't see her, but she was evidently close by. She picked up that thought. *I am invisible. The archers defending the castle are nervous about flying dragons.*

So she stayed out of their sight. That made sense. "Then some other mechanism," I said to Dubi. "A balloon, or magically floating platform."

"That might be," he said thoughtfully. "In the confusion of the moment I did not think to search for any such artifact, and by the time things settled, it was too late."

"So it could have been a normal archer, supported by a rogue wizard," I said.

"It could have been," he agreed. "Or a rogue noble with a bound wizard."

"Like Lord Mephisto."

"Like Lord Mephisto," he echoed grimly.

But I suspected it would not be as simple as that. The obvious suspect is not always the real culprit.

"The princess," I said, now that I had him alone. "Why did the king adopt her?"

"I have pondered that myself," he said. "I conjecture that he was becoming isolated, by the assassinations and his own choice, and wanted someone to sustain him in his old age, as a mistress would not."

"He wanted to be loved," I said.

"Yes. Not for his power, not to curry favor, but for himself. So he started with a child, a baby, and did everything for her. Also—" He faded out thoughtfully.

"There was something about her," I prompted.

"There was indeed. She was a remarkably pretty baby, and grew into a beautiful woman, as you may have noticed."

"I noticed."

"But it was also the magic. The magic of royals tends to be personal, sometimes subtle. Her kiss—"

"Even as a baby?"

"Even as a baby, it was remarkably evocative. He saw her, picked her up, she kissed him, and he took her home and adopted her. That kiss established that there was royalty somewhere in her ancestry, making her legitimate."

I had an ugly thought, but it had to be explored. "So she seduced him, in her way, making him love her."

"Yes. She was always a remarkable comfort to the king."

"Could she have been planted?"

Evidently the translation spell took that literally. "People do not grow like trees."

"I mean, could she have been placed in the king's way by some other party, so that he would see her and be smitten by her, and thus that other person would have an unwitting agent close to the king? Perhaps to assume the throne?"

He shook his head. "I do not like this thought at all. But it never occurred to me. This is perhaps one reason we need you: to think in ways we have not. Yet the princess is absolutely loyal. I can't believe that she would ever betray the interests of the king, or the kingdom. She worshiped him, and reflected his interest in good governance. She is also a fine person in her own right."

I did not like this line of speculation either, and was glad to know the princess was as nice as she seemed. But I had a job to do. "She would not betray him consciously," I said. "But if there were some avenue to her mind, planted, I mean set up in her infancy, that another person could use, he might cause her to think that his directives were her own thoughts. She could become the unconscious agent of a foreign power."

"This is sickening! But must be considered. Yet why try to assassinate her, if this were the case?"

"To make it look as if she is another potential victim. So that no one would suspect her. Eliminate all the legitimate claimants to the throne, so that she alone remains, then use her to govern the kingdom as the regent of an unknown master."

He looked at me. "I hate this. The princess never kissed me, but I do love her. Such a thing would be an utter horror."

I knew how that was. "I don't like the notion much either. But I have to consider it. It's my job."

"It is a necessary job," he said distastefully. "Like cleaning out the piss-pot. What else do you require?"

"Who took care of the princess when she was young? Before the nanny? There must have been a woman. She may know something."

"The Matron," he agreed. "I shall summon her now."

"What's her name?"

"She surely has one, but it's been lost in time. She is simply Matron." He snapped his fingers, and a stout middle-aged woman appeared. "This is Roan, whom we fetched from Earthside. He is investigating the king's demise. Cooperate." Dubi departed.

Matron oriented on me, her glower developing. She was evidently cooperating under duress. "We don't like snoops here."

I fixed her with my gaze. "I am here to find out who assassinated the king, so that we can bring that person to justice. I have learned that he was slain by an arrow on the balcony. Do you know anything about that?"

"Who did it? No. But I was the first to reach him. I was cleaning up here when I heard him groan and went to him. I was surprised, of course, as the king has a fear of heights. Almost never did he venture onto the balcony."

"Then why was he there at the time of his death?"

"I suppose that is for you to find out, snoop. Anyway, it was only a minute or so, but already too late. He had been pierced through the heart. I summoned the guards immediately, but they found nothing. The assassin had gotten away."

"Naturally you saved his clothing, and the arrow."

"Naturally. I did not clean them, lest I obliterate some evidence of the source of the attack."

"That was wise. Did you see anything outside?"

"It was dark."

Was that an evasion? "Was there anything? A light, an odor, a sound?"

"Nothing. I have no idea where that arrow came from. It was as if it had been magicked out of thin air."

"That is possible," I agreed. "That would eliminate the need for a bowman nearby."

"Are we done here?" she asked, plainly resenting my intrusion.

"Not quite. You took care of the princess?"

"Leave her out of this," she snapped. "Her grief is bad enough without being stirred by outsiders."

"It is just barely possible that she is part of the plot against the king," I said evenly.

"Never!" she flared. "You're an ass and a scoundrel to even think it! She was always the perfect child and the perfect young woman, and she adored the king. Now get out of here before I lose my temper."

Her attitude was starting to get to me. I reacted as I tend to, with similar ire. "Not until my job here is done. I think you know something."

"You accuse *me*?" she demanded, furious.

"No. I simply want to know what you know, so I can do my job. What aren't you telling me?"

"Nothing." She turned to go.

I stepped quickly to cut her off. I stared her hard in the face, assuming my best interrogative manner. "Tell me."

Her mouth opened in the beginning of a snarl. Then it froze. Then it transmuted to wonder. Then something else. "Gods of Hell!" she swore softly.

"What?" I asked, annoyed.

"My Lord! You've got it!"

"Got what?"

"You're royal!"

I remembered Dubi's narration of my father's origin. "By a bastard route, maybe. But that's not relevant to this investigation."

"You're in line to be king! Oh my lord, I apologize for doubting you."

"What are you talking about?"

Matron recovered some of her equilibrium. "You don't know, do you!"

"You are being clear as mud."

"The royals—they all have magic. Mostly subtle, but devastatingly effective when they choose to use it. The princess can reduce a man to jelly by kissing him. Your power is similar, only it's in your eyes. You have the love stare."

"The what?"

"You can look into a woman's eyes and seduce her. You must have had your sudden conquests, back where you came from. That's your magic."

I thought about the cheating wives I had tailed, and wound up cheating with myself. It had seemed natural at the time, but now I wondered: had I unconsciously compelled them with my stare? Magic did work on Earth, when brought there, as I had seen. That would explain a lot. She was probably right about me. "I didn't know," I said somewhat lamely.

"You thought it was your personal charm? You're charming as an angry scorpion! But you've got the power. I'd get into bed with you now, if you asked." She shuddered. "Please don't ask."

"I—won't ask," I said. "I apologize for using my—my power on you. I thought I was interrogating you." As I had interrogated women in the past. When they got really friendly I had supposed that maybe they were trying to distract me from awkward questions. Now I realized that it was more than that.

"Don't let the princess kiss you," she said. "That's what I wasn't telling you before." She didn't realize that I already knew that detail before I talked with her. "But be fair: don't compel

PIERS ANTHONY AND J.R. RAIN

her with your gaze. Keep it muted. Then maybe the two of you can work together to find the assassin." It was obvious that she no longer questioned my legitimacy.

"Fair enough," I said. I had a lot to process.

I left her and made my way down to the ground floor, where Dubi was waiting to intercept me. "You learned something!" he said, seeing my face.

"I learned something," I agreed. "But not what I expected."

CHAPTER SEVEN

I next asked to see the princess.

Dubi obliged, summoning her magically. I waited in what Dubi called the Dragon Room. Tapestries of the creatures hung from the walls, many of them depicting a beautiful creature flying high above the ground. This creature did not look like Fiera. Bigger, more fierce. More images of dragons were in the many of the room's stained glass windows. The Dragon Room indeed.

The princess came in a moment later as I was gazing up at another such tapestry. This one depicted a massive beast flying low over a castle, and belching a long plume of fire.

The princess came to me, her eyes cast down, her hands folded in front of her. I said, "Thank you for coming."

"Dubi asked me to cooperate with you."

"I'm here to help," I said. "To the best of my abilities."

"And what are your abilities?" She continued looking down.

"Finding bad guys."

"You are an investigator, I'm told."

"It's a living," I said.

"Investigating crimes is what you do for a living?"

"Not always crimes," I said. "Sometimes I'm hired to gather information for my clients."

"I see," she said, and stepped over to me, and gazed up at the tapestry. "You snoop for a living."

"I'm a helluva good snoop."

"So you say," she said, and I sensed she was being playful. "Why have you summoned me, Sir Roan?"

"I have questions for you."

She turned her head to look at me, but I shifted my gaze lower, to her slender neck, her bared shoulders, to the way her embroidered blouse fit her snugly.

"So ask them?" she said.

Admittedly, I found myself distracted by the curves of her body; in particular, her rounded chest. I had not realized that the beautiful princess also possessed a beautiful body.

I swallowed and reminded myself that she was, in fact, my adopted aunt, even though I knew that was a stretch. After all, I had no idea that I had another family in the Realm. And, perhaps more importantly, she wasn't blood related.

She's still your dad's stepsister, I thought.

That was, of course, assuming that I hadn't lost my mind completely, which I suspected I had. Or, more likely, in the middle of the world's most vivid dream.

"How old were you when you were adopted by the king?"

"I was three and a half."

"Do you have any memory of your parents?"

"I only have a memory of a great fire and screaming and weeping, and, finally, the smell of burned flesh. It is, in fact, my first memory."

Jesus, I thought. I nearly asked Fiera to verify her claim for me, until I remembered the dragon was loyal to the princess first and foremost.

True, came Fiera's thought.

And then it occurred to me that Fiera had, undoubtedly, reported to the princess on the validity of my own thoughts and intentions.

Indeed, Sir Roan. She is aware that you find her highly desirable, and that you have a newfound awareness on your personal magic. I have warned her to avert her eyes from yours.

But she just looked at me—
I warned her, true, but she wanted to see for herself. I remind you
again, human, to treat my mistress with respect. Any manipulation on
your part will end tragically for you.
Jesus, I thought.
I doubt your deity will intervene. The princess also knows that your
father was the bastard child of the king, her adopted father. She is aware
of your internal struggle.
Is anything private? I asked, exasperated.
Not between me and the princess, human.
Enough. I decided to close my thoughts for the moment. I
needed to know my thoughts were safe—and all my own.

"What's your name?" I asked, realizing I'd only been calling
her "the princess."

"Rose," she said. She'd gone back to gazing up at the tapestry.

"Princess Rose," I said. "Very beautiful."

"Thank you, Sir Roan."

I swallowed. Her voice had a musical lilt to it. I remembered
Dubi's own voice back before he'd used the translation spell. He
had sounded as if he were singing. I detected some of that now
in the princess's voice.

So beautiful, I thought.

"Where did you live prior to being adopted by the king?"

"An orphanage. It was terrible."

"I'm sorry to hear that," I said, and couldn't imagine the con-
ditions of a medieval-type of orphanage.

I saw her nod. She reached out and touched the frayed hem
of the tapestry. She had long and slender fingers. She wore a sil-
ver ring on her thumb...a ring with a carved image of a dragon.

"It wasn't so bad. A man came to visit me often. He was kind
to me."

Bingo, I thought. "What else do you remember about him?"

"He taught me magic, and would often sit with me for long
periods teaching me various illusions."

I was about to ask what kind of illusions, when a flame appeared before my eyes. It danced briefly, then disappeared in a puff of smoke.

She giggled shyly next to me and bumped me with her hip, which sent a shiver of pleasure through me. She said, "That was my first trick."

"So you are a witch, too?" I asked.

"Potentially, but that is not the path I have found myself on. I am first a royal."

"I see. Do you have any other memories of this man? What is his name?"

"He never told me his name. I called him uncle."

"What did he look like?"

"A long beard. Piercing blue eyes. A smile always on his lips. He was so kind to me."

"Have you ever seen him again?"

She released the hem of the tapestry and sighed deeply. "Yes and no."

"What do you mean?"

"I dream of him often."

"Tell me about your dreams."

"He comes to me often and apologizes. Always apologizing."

"For what?"

"I do not know."

"You miss him," I said. It wasn't a question. I heard it in her voice.

"Often."

"Do you have any other memories of him?"

"Only good memories. Kind memories."

"And that was when the king came for you?"

"Yes."

I was tempted to put my arm around her and console her, as I felt her sadness. But I didn't know what was acceptable protocol when dealing with a royal. More important, I didn't want an instant tan from Fiera.

Instead, I pointed to the tapestry, and the image of the dragon setting fire to a castle. "Some dragons are cruel?"

She giggled. "Perhaps, but this is the Dragon King."

I blinked. "Dragon King?"

"The Dragon King is a bedtime story we tell our kids here in the Realm, although many believe it is more than a bedtime story."

"I don't understand."

"Well, according to our legends, the Dragon King will descend upon high—a mountain some believe—and lay waste to our enemies. It is said that he will come when the land most needs him. There are some who hold out hope for him, especially now."

"And do you, too?" I asked. "Hold out hope?"

She looked away. "Yes."

"Well, that's quite a bedtime story indeed," I said, and pointed to the burning castle. "And this here..."

"Would be our enemy."

I nodded, and looked at her—but not into her eyes. No, not yet. And perhaps never again. Instead, I focused on her full lips, especially the fatter lower lip that was presently gleaming wet. I swallowed.

"Where were you on the night of your father's assassination?"

"Am I a suspect, Sir Roan?"

"I don't want you to be—but everyone, at this point, is a suspect."

Those lips smiled. Those magically delicious lips. I suddenly wanted her to kiss me, badly. I wanted to feel those lips on my own. I could do it, too. I needed only to look into her—

Down boy, I thought. *Today is not a good day to die.*

She said, "I was asleep in my bedroom."

"Was, ah, anyone with you?"

"Do I have an alibi, you mean?"

"Er, yes."

"And you ask if I was with, perhaps, a lover?"

I felt myself blushing mightily. Not common for me. As an investigator, I have asked far more intimate questions. But here, now, with a beautiful princess, I felt my face burning with embarrassment.

What's come over you? I asked myself. "Yes, I suppose," I managed to say.

Her lips curled up mischievously. "No, Sir Roan, Master Investigator. I was alone. I am, of course, a virgin."

The embarrassment turned into sweats, and I might as well have been a silly school boy with his first crush. 'I, um, see…" My voice trailed off.

She giggled some more. "You are cute, Sir Roan. Never have I seen a man blush so brightly."

"I, um, maybe I'm coming down with something."

"Perhaps. Perhaps not."

I needed to change the subject before I completely fell apart here. "Do you recall anything suspicious on the day of your father's assassination?"

"Suspicious how?"

"Anything out of the norm? Anything that struck you as odd?"

"No…except—" She stopped.

"Except what?"

"It's really nothing."

"Please, it might be important."

"It was just a dream."

"A dream?"

She nodded. "Just a silly dream I had the night before his death."

"Did you mention the dream to Dubi? To anyone?"

"No, of course not. It was just a silly dream."

"Tell me about it."

"I dreamed of a fleeing figure."

"Who was he?"

"I do not know."

"Where was he fleeing to?"

She took my hand and led me across the room and pushed open a window. She pointed beyond the castle. Below, a dense forest surrounded the castle and spread as far as the eye could see.

"Into the forest?" I asked.

She shook her head, and now I followed her pointing finger to what appeared to be a distant, conical mountain that belched steam. It was, by all appearances, an active volcano. "He fled to the mountain?" I asked.

"The Mountain of Fire, yes."

"Was the fleeing figure your father's assassin?"

"I do not know."

I stared at the smoking, distant mountain. "Does anyone live there?"

"Indeed."

"Let me guess," I said. "Lord Mephisto."

"Why, Sir Roan, you *are* an ace detective."

"When was your father killed?"

"Two nights ago."

"How long is the journey to the Mountain of Fire?"

"Four or five days on horseback—surely, you aren't giving much weight to my dream, Sir Roan."

I was, admittedly, torn. Any good investigator wouldn't give any consideration to a dream. Then again, most detectives didn't find themselves magically transplanted into a magical land.

Having studied the scene of the crime, I was certain that only an archer who was magically held aloft could have committed the crime. A lone archer, no doubt. The bolt held some evidence of being magically tampered with, as well. So, was there perhaps two of them? Wizard and assassin? Or were they one and the same? Or had the wizard stayed behind, while the assassin fled?

I didn't know, but I was beginning to think that there might be something to Princess Rose's dream. A dream she'd never divulged until now. In this business, I've learned to trust my hunches. And my hunch told me now to follow-up on the princess's dream.

Fiera, I thought, opening up my thoughts once again. *Find me Dubi.*

Found him. He's on the way.

A moment later, the old wizard stepped into the Dragon Room, and I told them my plan.

CHAPTER EIGHT

"There are two stages of my plan, such as it is," I told them. "First we four go to the forest nearest the turret where the king was killed, because there is likely to be evidence of someone recently there. A bowman or a mage, or both. Ground support. That evidence will implicate Lord Mephisto. Then I will go see Lord Mephisto for a candid dialogue."

Princess and Wizard both stared at me as if I had lost what little wit I had. "Surely you jest," Dubi said after a moment.

"Not at all," I assured them.

What a ploy! Fiera thought. I had forgotten to shield my mind. I hastily remedied that. *You can come too,* I thought to her. *You're one of the four.*

"How can you know what we'll find, before we check?" Rose asked.

"And if Lord Mephisto is guilty, it would be absolute folly to place yourself in his hands with any such charge," added Dubi.

I eyed them both. "You hired me for a job. Are you going to let me do it?"

Rose and Dubi exchanged a weary glance. "We can at least check the forest," the princess said.

"But we had best summon the guards," Dubi said.

"No. Too many people will likely mess up the evidence. Just us."

Dubi winced, but let it be. "At least we'll have Fiera."

More than sufficient, the dragon thought smugly.

We went to the forest. It was larger from the ground than it had looked from above. The trees reached up in stately columns, with branches spreading out to intercept most of the sunlight before it had a chance to warm the forest floor. There were only a few straggling bushes, most of them starved out by the gloom. Even so, it was not safe for Fiera to fully spread her wings. She would be ground-bound here.

"What are we looking for?" Dubi asked.

"Scuff marks," I said. "Dropped items. Anything that some- one might have inadvertently lost in the darkness."

"There's a lot of ground to cover," Rose said. "Maybe we should separate and each of us check sections."

"No," Dubi said immediately. "Separation in the field is dangerous."

"Then make two parties," Rose said. "I will go with Roan. You go with Fiera."

Dubi glanced at the dragon, who made a rippling shrug, going along with it. That was interesting, as she was bound to the princess. We separated, moving left and right along the edge of the forest.

Soon we were out of sight of the other two. "Exactly why are we here?" Rose asked me, stepping enticingly close.

"Well, it's called crime scene investigation. Sometimes the smallest things can have enormous significance."

"That's interesting," she said. Her lovely face was only inches from mine.

"But we have to examine the ground and the tree trunks," I said. "Not each other."

Then she kissed me. It caught me entirely off guard. Suddenly her soft lips were pressing into mine, paradise in my face.

I jerked away. "What are you doing? I don't want to be your love slave!"

She laughed. "Silly, I don't have to enslave every man I kiss, any more than you have to compel every woman you look at. Sometimes a kiss is just a kiss. That one was just for fun. You are not my love slave."

"That's what you think," I muttered. "You don't need to use magic on me to do it."

"I'm sorry," she said contritely. "I just wanted to get you alone so I could have my little way with you."

Little way? So she had maneuvered to make the separate parties. Never underestimate the cunning of a woman!

You're not the only one with devious plans, Fiera thought, amused. Now I understood why the dragon had agreed to separate from the princess; she had been in on that one.

"Why?" I demanded as my feelings circled for a landing that I feared would be more like a crash.

"Because I like you. Do I need any other reason?"

"Yes! You're the princess. You can't afford to waste yourself on just any man."

"Indeed, and I do not. But it is becoming apparent that you are not just any man," she said evenly. "You have as much of a claim to the throne as I do."

"I'm the son of a bastard!" I protested.

"And I'm adopted. So both bloodlines are compromised. We might conclude that it is better to merge them and eliminate any question of legitimacy."

"Merge the lines? As in marriage? What about love?"

She stared at me blankly. "How does love relate?"

It seemed that we had a cultural difference here. "Where I come from, folk marry for love, not lineage. Generally."

Rose shook her head. "This is not the rule with royals. Marriage is a tool to secure advantage and lineage. The sex can be fun, too, before he gets too many concubines. It does help if the participants come to like each other, in time. But that is hardly the point."

I was appalled. "Princess! This is not—"

I couldn't finish, because she cut me off with another kiss. This one had just enough more *oomph* so that I knew she was applying a touch of her magic. This time I didn't jerk away; I couldn't. I wanted to remain this way forever. She was a complete dream.

She finally let me loose. "Now that we have established that, let's see what else we can find," she said, smiling.

I was satisfied to agree. I couldn't withstand any more of her kisses, even if they supposedly lacked magic. If she meant to establish who was to be the dominant member of this association, she had accomplished it. But it bothered me to think she was merely being practical. That the burgeoning emotion she stirred in me was only a ploy to make me behave.

Rose continued the search, smiling obscurely.

Then again, maybe she was looking for love with a qualified man, rather than endure the arranged marriage that otherwise threatened. That put a more positive face on it.

Found something, Fiera's thought came.

We hurried to rejoin the others. There was a swatch of torn cloth hung up on a thorny bush. There was part of a monogram on it: EPH.

"Mephisto," I said.

"You knew we would find it," Dubi said.

"I thought it likely." But this was so obvious it was clumsy. Someone evidently took me for a fool.

"Now with this proof of his guilt you want to brace him in his den?" Rose asked.

"Making yourself the perfect target?" Dubi added.

"Of course," I agreed.

Rose looked at Dubi. "Should I kiss him?" Meaning to subjugate me so that I could no longer contemplate going against her preference.

"We do not enjoy feeling stupid," Dubi said. "Please explain your reasoning. Why were you so sure this evidence would be found here, and why are you determined to put your head in the noose? Fiera thinks you do have reason."

"Just this," I said. "Mephisto is not our man. He is being crudely framed, in the hope that we will go after him and either kill him or get killed ourselves. The real assassin is trying to trick the good guys into knocking each other off. That will make it that much easier to take over the kingdom with apparently clean hands."

"Framed," Dubi said thoughtfully. "You have more indication of this?"

"Yes. When we were ambushed by the bandits, they had been set up. We took one prisoner, and he was the one who recognized the spy as one of Lord Mephisto's minions. That was entirely too coincidental and convenient, and not because of any artifice on Boffo's part; he would not deceive the princess. Some one else must have set that spy on us, possibly with a fake message to the spy that it was Mephisto's directive. Knowing that Boffo would recognize him, and if we happened to catch him, he would implicate Mephisto. Then I learned from you that Mephisto was already your leading suspect. There must have been other things you picked up on that implicated him. Again, suspiciously convenient. It is possible that he is the one, but I think more likely that he is not. That's why I have to talk to him directly. If he is innocent, he will not be pleased about the frame."

"And if he is guilty?"

"He is unlikely to off me in his own castle. That would confirm his guilt. So I am probably safer there than elsewhere. In any event, it should be an interesting interview that will tell me more than his words do."

"More?" Dubi asked.

I glanced at Rose. "It is possible that Lord Mephisto is your apologetic uncle, who visited you first personally, then in your dreams. That he knows you are a target for assassination, and feels guilty for allowing you to be out there alone, as it were, but he can't make his case without alerting the true assassin to the suspicion. That he loves you and wants to protect you, but is largely unable."

"Uncle!" she said, amazed.

"This is too much of a risk," Dubi said. "You are a claimant to the throne yourself. If he is guilty, he may not be able to resist assassinating you. That would leave just one other to remove."

"Does anyone besides you, Rose, and Fiera know about my claim?"

"We think not," Dubi said.

"So to Mephisto I should be a snooping hireling not worth eliminating."

Once more the wizard and the princess exchanged glances. Neither of them was comfortable with this.

Neither am I, Fiera thought. *A telepath could have snooped on your unguarded mind.*

"But if we do nothing, we may be sure that the assassin, whoever he is, will not be idle. He'll be coming after one or more of us on his own schedule. Better to keep moving, keep him off-guard. So now please let me do what you hired me for. I need to interview Mephisto."

"There is a certain twisted logic there," Dubi said reluctantly. "I can't go there; there are wards against wizards. But you could."

Rose sighed. "In that case, go, Sir Roan. I will go with you."

"No!" Dubi and I said almost together, and I felt Fiera's mental flare.

"You like logic?" Rose said defiantly. "Then assimilate this: if Mephisto is 'Uncle,' only I will be able to fathom his illusion and recognize him. And if he should threaten me or you, I can kiss him. But I think he won't. As you say, assassinating me in his own castle would advertise his guilt and rouse the entire kingdom against him. I should be as safe there as you. And if he is innocent, there's no danger anyway, and we may gain a powerful ally."

Got you there, the dragon thought. *I can't go either, because of the dragon wards.*

I was not completely pleased, but her logic, based on mine, was as good as mine. "Then it is time to go see Lord Mephisto," I said. "How do we get there pronto?"

Dubi looked as if he had swallowed a rotten egg. "I have a method."

"Good enough. Let's be on our way."

CHAPTER NINE

D ubi showed us into another room.

This one was down a long flight of stairs and through a narrow tunnel, where we stepped into what I figured was Dubi's personal voodoo room. Or whatever he called it. I saw caged birds and animals of all shapes and sizes. What he did with these animals, I didn't know, but I hoped nothing too nefarious.

There was an actual cauldron that sat near a fire. I stepped over to it and peered inside, hoping like crazy not to see something too traumatizing. The smell that wafted out of it was... heavenly. Dubi walked up next to me, and patted my back. I jumped, despite myself.

"Dinner," he said, smiling. He used a ladle to mix in a colorful array of vegetables and what appeared to be chunks of red meat. "The equivalent of your beef stew."

I nodded, relieved. What a high-level wizard did in his private chambers was enough to make my imagination run wild. Too wild.

"Looks good," I said.

"You must be famished."

I thought about that, and had no clue when I might have eaten last. I agreed, and soon bowls and spoons were produced and the three of us spent a few quiet moments talking amicably and feasting on what turned out to be something utterly delicious.

"This meat..." I started, but Dubi shook his head.

"Not meat, my friend. We here in the Realm do not approve of the killing and eating of our animals. The meat is a magical mixture of plant proteins."

"Like soy," I said.

He cocked his head a little. Undoubtedly, his magical translation spell was doing its best to translate my word into the realm's equivalent. Finally, he nodded. "Indeed. Like soy."

Once finished, tankards of something that could have been beer—but was much sweeter, mead, perhaps—was produced. I had two.

Next, Dubi led us over to a stone archway that led...into a stone wall. "The portal," he said, and seemed proud.

"It's a wall," I said, and caught Princess Rose smiling next to me.

"In appearance only, Detective Roan. From this portal, I can send you anywhere in the realm. Well, anywhere within a few hundred clacks."

"It's not exact?"

"Heavens, no," he said jovially.

A sudden, alarming thought occurred to me. "What if we arrive, say, in a tree? Or within a mountain?"

"Then that would be most unfortunate," said the older wizard, grinning. He and the princess exchanged another grin.

Then he closed his eyes, waved his hand, and the stone wall shimmered...and disappeared entirely. Beyond lay a forest path, and beyond that, rising high above the forest, was another castle. This one appeared darker and more formidable than the castle I presently found myself in. Black smoke belched from a nearby volcano. The Mountain of Fire.

Dubi studied the portal, then shrugged. "Sadly, this is as close as I can get you. As you can see, you will not appear in a tree or a mountain or even a river. You are much more likely to come across one of Lord Mephisto's many patrols, than cutthroats and thieves."

With that, we were given provisions, satchels filled with cheese, bread and water skins. I took the princess's hand, and together stepped through the archway...and found ourselves on a forest trail.

I turned back, and could only see a winding trail disappearing into the thick foliage. There was no portal, or even Dubi. Powerful magic indeed!

We followed the path that led in the direction of the castle, I re-loaded my pistol. The princess watched me curiously. "A deadly weapon," she said.

"Too deadly. It causes much strife in my world."

"I can imagine. May I hold it?"

I frowned at that, and gently handed it over to her, advising her how to hold it as I did so. She took the Smith & Wesson carefully enough, turning it over and getting a feel for it. Then she aimed it a nearby tree and pulled the trigger.

The sound was deafening, and would surely alert any of Mephisto's nearby patrols. I was about to ask her why she'd acted so carelessly when something heavy fell from the tree. It was a man, and, from all indications, he had been shot in the heart. A crossbow clattered next to him.

Princess Rose walked up to him. The look on her face "A common thief," she said. "Not our assassin."

"Holy shit," I said, finally finding words. "How...how did you know?"

"When you grow up in the forests of the Realm, Detective Roan, you learn to look into the trees."

She handed me the pistol and moved on. I looked again at the dead man at my feet, at the perfectly placed shot over his heart, and found myself unable to make any sense of it. The bandit being right here where we jumped to the path, and the princess making such a shot.

Worse, was her attitude toward the dead man. Her apparent disdain for life.

She looked back and saw me standing over the alleged thief. "Make no mistake, Roan. He would have killed us without a second thought."

I considered the irony in her words as I caught up to her. I also considered the case of my father's own strange death. My father, Roan Senior, had been quite fit and healthy for his age. In fact, he was the picture of health. Which was why when he had been found dead in his Los Angeles home, all had been surprised. None more than me.

An autopsy had been performed, confirming initial suspicions: he'd died of a stroke. The evidence of a stroke wasn't conclusive, but it seemed the most likely. There had been no sign of foul play, and no signs of an accident. Maybe I was paranoid to remember how there were drugs that could enter the system and induce something like a stroke. A form of poisoning. It was a stock in trade in certain circles.

He'd been found by his cleaning lady. Who'd reported, interestingly enough, seeing a woman at my father's house just the night before. A young woman. A beautiful woman. My father had been fit for his age...and single. I was aware that he'd often dated well below his age group. After all, he was handsome and successful and well-off. Highly desirable traits to some women.

So the fact that a woman had been seen the night before his death had been curious, but not unlikely. The police never did locate her for questioning, which had always been frustrating to me, and undoubtedly so for the police themselves.

What occurred to me now was the housecleaner's eye witness statement. The woman had been tall with flowing strawberry blond hair. She'd also had, of all things, a pet lizard sitting on her shoulder. An iguana, undoubtedly. A curious fact that always puzzled the police. Hell, puzzled me, as well.

But as I followed the the princess along the narrow trail, I was suddenly well aware of her long legs and lightly tinted hair. The princess didn't have an iguana sitting on her shoulder.

But she certainly had a pet dragon.

We continued along in silence, and it wasn't long before we attracted the attention of a regiment of guards who escorted us rather rudely up to the ominous castle.

Where Lord Mephisto awaited.

CHAPTER TEN

The castle was smaller than the late king's residence, but similarly comfortable inside. The guards escorted us to an elaborate reception hall with ornate carved ivory chairs. Ivory? Those had to be huge elephants to provide tusks big enough to be carved into such furniture. More likely it was fake ivory designed to be impressive. Lord Mephisto wanted us to be daunted. And how would he himself appear? Like the wonderful wizard of Oz?

A man stepped forward to greet us as the guards retreated. He was middle aged, portly, with receding hair and slightly uneven teeth. His clothing was not impressive either; there was a button missing from his jacket, and his trousers had thin worn spots. "Good to meet you at last, Princess Rose," he said. "And you too, Roan Quigley." He took Rose's hand to kiss, then held out his hand to shake mine.

This was the formidable rival claimant to the throne? I took it in stride. "Lord Mephisto, I presume," I said as I shook his hand.

"Indeed." His fingers were somewhat flaccid; I was not impressed. Until I realized that he must be trying to fake us out. He wanted to come across as a pushover, when he was anything but. This was not his real appearance or manner. "Please be suitably seated," he said, gesturing to the chairs.

We obeyed, sitting beside each other, facing him. Rose crossed her legs, showing a fair length of thigh. She was trying to work her magic on him, but he seemed unaffected.

"We come on business," I said. "May we speak candidly?"

"Candor is a rare and precious quality," he said. "You may employ it, but I prefer caution." He snapped his fingers, and a uniformed maid appeared. "Serve our guests refreshments as we hold our dialogue."

The maid curtsied and departed. In a moment she returned with a large glass tray supporting goblets and sweetbreads.

"Thank you, but I think I am not hungry," Rose said somewhat tightly.

"Oh, my dear, do not be afraid to sample my wares," Mephisto said, looking pained. "If I meant you ill, I would hardly need to drug you. Believe me, I have nothing but the best of intentions toward you." He took a goblet and sipped, demonstrating its safety.

Well, might as well find out. I took a goblet and sipped similarly. The beverage tasted like sparkling burgundy. I have had some experience with knockout drops, and this seemed innocent. Of course it was impossible to tell by taste alone.

Rose relented and took her own goblet, then a sweetbread. She glanced at me.

I set myself and launched into it. "As you surely know, there is a problem with assassinations. Possible claimants to the throne are being systematically eliminated. The king himself died recently, and I have been hired to help find his killer and bring him to justice. You are a suspect."

"Of course I am," Mephisto agreed equably.

"We found evidence implicating you."

"Naturally. Yet you came here."

"Because it looks to me like a frame," I said. "I suspect that someone is trying to set claimants against each other, in the hope that they will do the assassin's dirty work for him. I think we may be natural allies. Do you agree?"

Mephisto made a gesture of indifference. "We all have somewhat clouded claims. We may be natural rivals."

He was arguing the other case? What was his game? "If the assassin is none of us," I continued doggedly, "we need to make common cause to discover him, and deal with him."

"Why do you assume the assassin is male?" he asked. "It may have been a female who took out your father."

If he was trying to set us back, he was succeeding. Rose quickly stood up as if discovering a tack in her chair, and I felt a clutch in my gut that wasn't from the food. "What do you know of this?"

"I have a certain interest," Mephisto said. "Because I am also a target. My retainers were against admitting the two of you to my presence, but I felt it was best to be direct. I have researched each and every assassination, including that of your father. I do not know whom the assassin may be, but merely point out that the evidence is inconclusive. That person was clearly trying to frame the princess herself."

"Me!" Rose exclaimed, stepping close to him.

Mephisto eyed her speculatively. "I gather you were not informed about that detail, my dear. The woman who took out mister Quigley looked very much like you, and so you also are a suspect."

"Me!" she repeated, reddening in anger.

"We spoke of candor," he reminded her.

She dived at him. It was not an attack, exactly. Instead she kissed him fast and hard. I would have cautioned her, but it had not occurred to me that she would do this at this stage. Now the fat was in the fire, maybe. She had delivered the love-slave kiss.

Rose drew back. "And what do you say now?" she asked.

Mephisto smiled. Then he reached out, caught her about the middle, drew her down so that she was across his knees, and spanked her smartly on the bottom. "Bad girl," he said.

My jaw literally dropped. Bemused, I could only watch as she scrambled back to her feet, glaring at Lord Mephisto. "How dare you! I am the princess!"

He laughed. "As you can see, your magic did not affect me. It couldn't."

"That's impossible," she spluttered. "How could you resist it?"

Then I caught on. "Because he is your father," I said.

She was astonished. "You can't be!"

"Perhaps you should assume your natural form now," I told Mephisto.

"Perhaps I should," he agreed. He shimmered, and became a lean man with piercing blue eyes and a long beard.

"Uncle!" she exclaimed.

"Father," he corrected. "Now that the secret is out." He glanced at me. "You are sharper than I anticipated. I had not meant to reveal that aspect."

"It's my business," I said gruffly. Then, to Rose: "You can't enchant him with magic he taught you, and even if you could, it would make no difference, because he is already your love slave—a very different kind of love, a father's love—and has been since your birth. He is not the assassin."

Evidently bemused, she focused on a detail. "Then what are you apologetic about?" she asked him. "You come to me in my dreams."

Mephisto looked away briefly. "I prefer to avoid that particular issue."

"No!" she said furiously. "You have humiliated me and I demand satisfaction."

"It's a fair case," I said, almost amused.

He sighed. "So it is. It is because your mother was the queen. You are a bastard, and I can never forgive myself for inflicting that status on you."

"The queen," she echoed, stunned. "Bastard?"

"There is more illicit sex than royalty likes to admit," Mephisto said. "The king had affairs, and so did the queen. With me, in fact…and perhaps others. We generally don't talk about such things, but we do keep track of the royal lines."

"My father was the child of the *king's* mistress," I added. "Sent to Earth for his supposed safety." I looked at Mephisto. "You are of his generation; why did you stay here?"

"I was not threatened at the time."

"Until the assassin caught on that you were the king's son by yet another mistress," I said, taking a calculated guess.

He nodded. "True. But by then I was able to protect myself."

"But then you had an affair with the king's young second wife. Your father's young second wife, in fact."

He looked away. "It was more complicated than that. She was my girlfriend first; I wanted to marry her. But the king had an eye for her, and she was flattered and went to him. Then it turned out she was already pregnant, and she died in childbirth soon after becoming queen. The baby was spirited away, to avoid embarrassment—Princess Rose, in fact—and I did what I could to help my daughter, unable to admit my true relationship to my little girl. Later the king got lonely and adopted her, knowing her origin, and of course I did not protest. She had a better life than I could give her. But I always loved her and sought to protect her in what indirect ways I could."

Rose resumed her seat. "My father," she whispered to herself, "was, in fact, my grandfather. I…I never knew."

"We all felt it best that you remain innocent," Mephisto said.

"All?" I asked alertly. "How many people were in on the secret?"

"Four. The king and I, Dubi, and Matron. All dedicated to the welfare of Princess Rose, the most likely heir to the throne." He glanced at me. "I do not want the throne. I want my daughter to have it. You will not find the assassin among us."

"What of the princess herself?" I asked. It was cruel, but I had to clear this. I wanted to believe in her innocence, but that business with my father had to be cleaned up.

"Never!" Rose snapped.

"You were not there with my father?" I asked her directly.

"I was not!" she said.

"Will you look me in the eye and repeat that?"

She was at a loss. "If I do that—"

"I will have power over you," I said. "But I will know."

She came to a decision. "I will do it. Then I will kiss you. Then we will have power over each other."

"Whenever you're ready," I said evenly, though I knew this was a crisis point. Yet that woman with my father…yes, I had to be sure.

She came to stand before me. She gazed into my face. I gave her the love stare. Or tried to. I still wasn't entirely sure how to do it, exactly. She blanched. Then she leaned down and kissed me on the mouth, and I felt our lips fairly crackle with magic energy. She was giving it her all, and it was potent as heaven and hell.

"There are other matters," Lord Mephisto said, and I realized that I had briefly lost consciousness. Rose was now sitting on my lap, her arm around my neck. We were both hopelessly in the thrall of love. But now I knew one thing: she was *not* the assassin. I had seen into her core and fathomed her innocence. She had seen into mine similarly. Love might have been a heavy price to pay, except that we had been heading there anyway.

"Other matters?" Rose asked, lifting her head.

"Three, in fact," Mephisto said. "First, as we know, we need to get serious about discovering the real identity of the assassin. Second, there is the dragon, Fiera."

"What about her?" Rose asked.

"Did you think she came from nowhere? That she's a natural dragon? She is a transformed sorceress the king arranged to protect you. She surely knows far more than she has told you, and it is time to learn what it is, because your life may depend on it."

Rose was silent, taken aback.

"And the third thing?" I asked.

"I have a certain magic sense." He smiled briefly. "It does run in the family. I know, to an extent, when a given person is alive or dead, particularly a friend or relative, even if I am not with him at the moment."

He had interpersonal magic, not a kiss or a stare, but an *awareness*. I could believe it. "Who is alive or dead?" I asked.

He paused briefly, then said, "The king. I should have felt it when he died; he is, after all, my father. I have not felt it. I suspect that he is still alive."

Rose and I stared at him. "But I saw his body," she said.

"You saw *a* body. Remember, he is the master of the dolls. It could have been a life-sized doll in his image. Those things can be made accurate even to internal organs. Dubi would have kept the secret. So would Matron."

"But *why?*" she asked.

"I think I can answer that," I said. "The king had—*has*—the same priorities we do. Mainly, to find the assassin. If in two generations the assassin remains active, it is obvious that more needs to be done. So maybe the king arranged to seem to die, thus removing himself from the picture and putting the issue of the inheritance of the throne at the forefront. The assassin has to act quickly now, or he will forfeit the throne by default. This should smoke him out. It is one bold play."

Mephisto nodded. "That is the way I see it. But I still have no idea who the assassin is."

"And you think Fiera the dragon might know?" I asked.

"She is thoroughly telepathic, and absolutely devoted to Rose," Mephisto said. "She knows the king and his situation. She might have been one of his mistresses before transforming. She might have information that she herself is unaware of, that we could interpret to identify the assassin. It's a weak path, but perhaps the best we have at the moment."

"It's a lead," I agreed. "And it's time to get on it, before the assassin strikes again."

"It is time," Rose agreed grimly. Then she glanced smokily at me and half smiled. "Dear."

And that was another situation that needed to be worked out, one way or another. Love was one thing, but as she had said, there's a lot more to royalty than that. For one thing, what good was love, if one or both of us died?

CHAPTER ELEVEN

M ephisto had a portal similar to Dubi.
"There are a few such portals in the Realm," he explained,
as he led us to a room in a turret high above. Or maybe it was a
castle keep. What the hell did I know? I was just a private dick
from Los Angeles.

Anyway, there was another such archway—similar to the one
in Dubi's potion room. Also in this room were paintings, and
these were of Mephisto himself, many of them showing his hunting prowess. In one, he was standing over what might have been
a bear, an arrow projecting from its heart region. There was also
another painting of the great dragon, what Rose had described
as the Dragon King. In this image, the great dragon was laying
waste to a great army. Dragon King indeed.

The room also appeared to be another potion room, of sorts.
Although not as profuse as Dubi's, it was clear that Mephisto was
no slouch. The man must certainly practice his share of magic,
whatever that meant, since I wasn't exactly sure how magic
worked.

"Many of the castles and fortresses are built over the portals,"
added Mephisto. "It makes transportation easier for royals and
nobility alike, not to mention escape when and if the castle is
under attack."

With that, the once-solid wall beyond the archway dissolved
into an open grass field. Beyond, I recognized what was the princess's less foreboding castle.

Princess Rose gave her father a final, curious look. Curious, at least to me. Was that regret in her eyes? Sadness? Or a silent signal?

Either way, both nodded subtly, and together we slipped through the portal.

We might as well have walked through a normal doorway—and not a magical one. With a simple step we were through the portal and standing in the field. I turned quickly, but saw only an endless expanse of gently blowing grass…and a quickly descending dragon from above. I gasped.

It's just me, human, thought Fiera.

Indeed, Princess Rose clapped once and rose up on her tiptoes, holding her hands out to the rapidly descending dragon. They shared a private exchange, and I was reminded again of how much my world had been changed, when I watched a woman I cared for—heck, loved—nestle with a flying serpent.

I'm not in Kansas anymore, I thought. *Or Los Angeles.*

Once girl and dragon had been re-united, and greetings warmly expressed, I asked Fiera if we could ask her a few questions. The dragon looked at me sharply, snapping its triangular head up from where it had been nuzzling the princess, reminding me very much of a horse and her girl.

The dragon paused and I knew it was scanning my thoughts rapidly. I kept them open for now.

Its great head seemed to nod once. *I guess the cat is out of the bag,* she said, and I nearly smiled at the use of the popular American idiom, recognizing that it was Dubi's translation magic at work.

You were once human, I said.

It nodded again, a very human gesture, then lowered its long neck. "Climb aboard, and I will tell you about it on the flight back."

"Climb aboard?" I asked, but Princess Rose was already throwing a leg over the dragon's narrow neck.

"Sit behind me, love," she said, patting the spot directly behind her.

I worked up some nerve, reminded myself that I was a fearless detective, and swung a leg over the dragon's slender neck. Slender, yes, but incredibly strong. I felt it tense beneath me as the creature lifted its head.

"Hang on!" shouted Princess Rose, and I did, wrapping my arms tightly around her narrow waist—and trying to ignore just how perfect her body felt—even as she curled her own arms around the dragon's scaly neck.

With that, the great beast ran forward on lumbering, slightly awkward legs, then beat its wings once, twice, and soon we were air born. But not by much. We flew low to the ground at first, brushing the tall grass, as Fiera, I suspected, adjusted to the added weight. Then with the flapping of her mighty wings we gained altitude. A good thing, too, as the surrounding forest was rapidly approaching.

I instinctively raised my legs as we just clipped the tallest trees and soon we were racing into the sky. The nearly-hysterical laughter I heard was my own, as this was thrilling beyond anything I could have ever imagined. I was flying, flying. Just a few days ago—or was it earlier today—worried about my alimony payment, and now...

Now I was flying.

And holding tightly to a woman that I now loved more than I had ever loved another woman. Yes, it was the enchantment at work, certainly, but the feeling was already there. The enchantment only flamed it to life.

Below, the ground sped by. Vibrant green forests, open meadows, rolling hills. A river snaked below, and also a winding road that cut through the countryside...all leading to the castle which rose up before us, far ahead.

I was a sorceress once, said Fiera, her words appearing in my head. She had waited, I suspected, for my own thoughts to calm down from the rush of flying. They surely hadn't calmed by much, but certainly enough to listen to her.

When? I asked. I suspected Fiera was relaying my own thoughts to Princess Rose, so that we could listen in to the telepathic conversation.

Just prior to Rose's birth. Lord Mephisto was right in one sense, but wrong in another. I was a mistress, yes, but not of the king.

Who then? I asked, feeling as if I were prying. Then again, that's exactly what private eyes do: they pry, asking the uncomfortable questions. But I knew the answer just as I asked it. *Lord Mephisto,* I said.

Very good, Detective Roan of Earth.

I was confused. *He thought you were most likely the mistress to the king.*

He thought wrong.

Then why would he suggest such a thing if, in fact, you had once been his mistress?

A good question to ask Lord Mephisto.

Surely he knows we would learn the truth, that you were, in fact, his mistress... and not the king.

Not necessarily, said Fiera.

She flapped her wings hard and we shot up through a low hanging cloud and burst above it. The dragon's wings flapped calmly, smoothly, powerfully. Below, the Realm disappeared beneath a sea of foamy clouds.

Help me understand, I said, wondering what Princess Rose was making of this.

I'm as confused as you, came Rose's reply.

Apparently, Fiera's open line of communication was working on many levels.

Let me explain, the dragon responded. *Yes, I was Mephisto's lover. One of his many lovers, in fact. I taught him the magic that he uses to this day. I loved him, but he did not love me. He had love for only one other.*

The queen, I thought.

The dragon nodded. *Indeed. She wasn't yet queen yet. She was a royalty, yes, the equivalent of your duchesses. She wasn't the queen until the king married her.*

When the king stole her from Lord Mephisto, I thought.

Indeed. The king was not aware, of course, that his prized young queen was already with child.

With Princess Rose, I thought.

Correct. He was, of course, furious when she showed early signs, proof that the young babe was not his. He banished her from the kingdom… and that proved fatal to our young queen.

I heard Princess Rose gasp, for we were, after all, speaking of her mother…her deceased mother. I squeezed her comfortingly.

The young queen was beyond the care of the realm's finest physicians—and even Dubi could not reach her in time. When her birth came, unexpectedly early, she perished. The babe lived, of course.

The babe had grown into a beautiful woman, I knew. A woman presently in my arms. Rose was silent, and I respected that.

Lord Mephisto's anger knew no bounds. His hatred for the king was nearly overwhelming, and that's when he enchanted me, to not only watch over the babe, but to watch over the king himself. And the Realm.

And report back to him, I added.

Indeed, Detective Roan.

Which is why he felt confident that you would give us any information he wanted you to relay to us, thinking you worked for him.

He was confident of this, yes.

I didn't know much about magic, but I was getting the hang of this. I thought: *Lord Mephisto is unaware that you have broken the spell.*

Recently broken, Fiera corrected. *Lord Mephisto had hoped to mislead you.*

Why? I asked, but suddenly knew the answer. I nodded. *Because he killed the king.*

Or thought he had, added Princess Rose, her soft thoughts joining the conversation for the first time.

Indeed, said the dragon. *And he searches for the king to this day, hoping to finally avenge the death of his one true love. I was, in effect, his eyes and ears within the Realm—and over the Realm. And let me assure you, Lord Mephisto is planning a great assault. The ultimate act of revenge.*

Then why kill my father? I thought.

He was afraid of your father.

I don't understand, I thought.

He thought your father was the Dragon King. He was mistaken.

But a woman was last seen with my father.

Do you not recall that Lord Mephisto is a master of disguises? I was with him when your father was poisoned. I regret my participation greatly.

You were coerced, I heard myself say, although the words mostly faded away. My father had been poisoned. I clenched my fists and took a very deep breath. There was going to be hell to pay.

Princess Rose touched my shoulder and I felt her great love and empathy. We had both lost much in our lives—the shocking news of which we'd only recently learned.

After a moment, as the clouds cleared and the castle came into view—and after I had collected myself—I asked the dragon: *You are choosing to remain a dragon?*

I can, of course, shape-change at will. There are some of us who have this natural talent. Lord Mephisto saw the possibilities within me, which is why he chose me to watch over the princess and the Realm.

But you were his prisoner, his slave, said Princess Rose, her thoughts filled with grief.

His familiar, as he chose to put it. But I am a prisoner no more.

We began our decent, heading toward the castle's upper ramparts. Wind thundered over my ears and I held the princess closely. Perhaps a little too closely. Her warm body pushed back against my own. Uh oh. Below, the dragon's massive shadow caused a fair bit of panic as villagers looked up—then scattered. I would have thought they would be used to seeing Fiera by this point, until I recalled she mostly stayed invisible—which undoubtedly served Lord Mephisto's plans well.

As we glided down, we swept past the king's wide balcony— only just a few dozen feet away, in fact. Surely close enough to have gotten a shot off for an expert huntsman such as Lord Mephisto, I figured, thinking back to his hunting portraits.

You were compelled to carry Lord Mephisto, I said to Fiera, *when he killed the king—or thought he had killed the king.*

The dragon didn't say anything at first, and as Princess Rose and I scrambled off the creature's back, Fiera turned and looked back, her round, golden eyes regarding me silently. Finally, she nodded. *It was then that I made the decision to finally break the spell—it would be the last act the bastard compelled me to do. But first I needed help to break the spell.*

From Dubi? I asked.

She shook her head. *Dubi was unaware of my enchantment. Dragons can pair-bond with a human, especially royalty. And since I had no free will of my own, I could not speak in my defense. Indeed, I was a true prisoner in my own body, as the princess suggested.*

Then where did you find help? I asked.

From another. One of my own, in fact. Once I made telepathic contact with him, I found the courage—and the strength.

A fellow dragon? I asked, confused

She nodded. *It takes a dragon to know a dragon, although he is unaware of his great potential.*

Then he is a shape-shifter, too?

Of the highest order.

Princess Rose gasped. *You speak of the Dragon King!*

Perhaps, said Fiera, *although claiming his birthright will be up to him. Lord Mephisto thought he had killed the Dragon King on earth. But his information was wrong. His calculations were wrong. He wanted, in fact, the son.*

Both dragon and princess turned and looked at me.

CHAPTER TWELVE

"You can't be implying—" I said aloud. Both continued to gaze at me.

"But it's impossible! I'm from the *real* world. I mean, Earth, where magic and dragons don't exist. I was born there, lived there all my life."

"Your father was born here," Rose said. "He carried the royal blood. The Dragon King may have skipped his generation and manifested in his son, and now shown up there on Earth because, as you say, there is no magic there. It seemed like a safe refuge. But now you are here."

"That doesn't mean there's a dragon in me!"

"Not *in* you," she said patiently. "It would *be* you, transformed to human form. Hiding, waiting for the need to manifest. The need that we think now exists."

"I just can't believe—"

"Do I need to kiss you?"

That stopped me. There was hardly anything that would have pleased me more than her kiss, but this was not the time for it. "I'll think about it," I said. "Give me time."

She exchanged a glance with Fiera. "One night and day. We do have an assassin to deal with."

"Okay." At the moment I just wanted to get them both off my case.

Fiera faded out, and Princess Rose guided me into the castle. My mind was whirling, so that I was barely aware of where we went. It was as if I blinked, then found myself in a very nice room. "This

77

will be yours. You will want to refresh yourself," Rose said. "I will fetch you for the evening banquet in one hour." She walked away, her hips swaying gracefully.

Damn! They had hit me with an impossible concept. I had one day to come to terms with it, so that I could focus on my business here: to locate the king's assassin. Assuming the king was dead. No, wait—the assassin was Lord Mephisto! Or was it? I had only Fiera's word on that, and at this point I wasn't sure how far I could trust her. Her change of sides was a bit too facile for my taste. At least I had the wit to keep a tight clamp on my mind so that she could not read this doubt.

I stripped away my clothing and stepped into the shower, deliberately leaving the water cold. The shock of that clarified my mind acutely. One thought came to the fore: this whole thing was too pat. The way I had been fetched from Earth, introduced to the alluring princess, then the telepathic dragon, thrown into battle with the ambushing bandits, where Rose demonstrated her ability to kiss a man into love slavery, and Matron told me I had the Love Stare, meaning I was of royal descent, and meanwhile Boffo the love slave recognized a stalker as a minion of Lord Mephisto, who then turned out to be Rose's father, and the dragon was a transformed sorceress who claimed I was the Dragon King. All this was entirely too convenient, and it rang false. My training and inclination as a private eye readily saw the error of it, once shocked into action. It was more likely a complicated play performed for my dubious benefit. Was I a patsy, being set up to do something phenomenally foolish? Like claiming to be the Dragon King?

But what would be the point? Why would they waste time and put themselves at risk to journey to Earth to collect an ignorant private dick? Especially if the king wasn't really dead? That implied that I really was the Dragon King, or at least royal. Only they hadn't known that; the princess's surprise when the dragon said that was manifest.

I needed an objective opinion. And I knew where to get it.

I stepped out of the shower, dried on the plush towel provided, quickly got into the fresh clothing I found laid out for me, and sent out a limited thought. *Fiera!*

Yes, Roan, her answer came immediately.

I need to talk with Boffo Bandit. Privately. Where is he?

She did not question this. *Follow the red line.*

I looked. There before me was a red line on the floor. It went to the door. I followed out into the hall, down three flights of stone steps, and along a dusky back passage, where it ended. I stopped, not sure what to make of this. Then a castle servant walked across the hall, following an intersecting passage, without seeing me. After she passed, the line extended through that intersection. *You did say privately,* Fiera reminded me. So she had kept me out of sight.

Thanks, I thought, and resumed motion, my thoughts shielded again. The route led down two more flights into a network of cellars. I never would have found my way through this labyrinth on my own.

The line stopped outside a barred chamber. The gate was not locked. I pushed it open and entered. There was Boffo, sitting on a plank-board bench. "What in hades do you want, jerkoff?" he asked politely.

"You don't care whether I live or die," I said. "With a slight preference for die, right?"

"Right," he agreed. "And the princess isn't here to cough, so I don't have to cater to you at all. So smirk at my lodgings and move on, turd brain."

"So you can be completely objective about my situation," I said. "Because you *don't* care."

"What is your moronic point?"

"She kissed me too. I need your advice."

He burst into laughter. "And you thought you were special. Now you know."

"Now I am in deep doubt," I said. Then I launched into a summary of my situation, concluding "So it's too pat. I fear

I'm a fool. What do you recommend?" I had the distinct impression that he had already been familiar with my situation, which tended to confirm my suspicion that all this was an act.

"She thinks you're the Dragon King?" he asked, managing to suppress his mirth at the very notion. "First you better find out if it's true."

Which was actually a fair answer. "How?" Would he help, or evade?

"Well, maybe go see Mave."

"Who?"

"She's the scullery maid who sneaks me decent food from the kitchen. I'd screw her if I wasn't besotted with the princess at the moment; she's pretty enough. I'll be sorry as hades once the spell wears off and I'm out of here, knowing I could've had Mave. She's got the magic you need."

"The magic?" I asked blankly.

"She evokes dragons, dullard. That's her magic."

She evoked dragons! That was exactly what I needed. If she could not evoke mine, then that was false, and at least I'd know. He had, after all, given me good advice. "Thanks," I said. "What can I do for you in return?"

"You already saved my life, knot-head. What more do you want?"

So the bandit did have some minimal gratitude. "Maybe I can speak to the princess and get you better lodging."

"Don't bother. This is my style." Then he looked at me cannily. "But keep in mind that Mave will have her price, which you can't pay."

Her price? I decided not to follow up on that, as he obviously wanted to bait me further. He was enjoying this for some obscure reason. "We'll see." I departed.

The red line reappeared. Fiera knew where I was going next. Sure enough, it led to the kitchen. There in an alcove was a pretty girl touching up pastries on a table. She looked up, surprised, as I joined her. "Mave?"

"Yes, sir," she said, smiling. She had a cute face, flowing red hair and perfect teeth. Boffo was right: I would have liked to get to know her better, too, were I not already smitten by the princess.

"I am told I may be a dragon," I told her pointedly. "Can you evoke it? I promise not to toast or eat you if you do."

"Let me see, Sir Roan," she said. So she knew who I was. Word certainly got around within a castle. She stood, came to me, and put her hands on my head. The position put her nicely-filled decolletage under my nose so that I could see pretty near down through to Australia. "Oh, my!"

"There is something?" I asked, bemused.

"Oh, yes!" She took a truly impressive deep breath. "You are a dragon, all right, Sir Roan. But the spell is the most powerful I have encountered. I am normally a small dragon girl. This... this—"

"Is the Dragon King?" I prompted.

"It could be," she agreed, plainly awed. "It would exhaust me to evoke it, but I would do my utmost, if..."

Boffo had mentioned her price. "If what?"

"If you married me."

"What?"

"I am just a poor ignoble scullery girl," she said. "But I'd love to be a princess or a queen. The only way I'll ever be that is if I marry a prince or king. Then my peon lineage wouldn't matter. And if I got a child, it would be royal. That would be my dream realized."

I gazed at her, uncertain how to handle this.

"I promise I would not be a jealous wife," she continued. "You could have any other women you wanted, once you got me pregnant. I would stay out of your way so as not to embarrass you by my lowly origin. It would be no trouble at all for you. And if you liked me, I would do anything in bed that you wanted, no matter how bizarre. I would just be so grateful."

I sighed inwardly. Two days ago this would have been a fabulous offer. "I'm sorry, Mave," I said. "I can't marry you. The princess kissed me."

"Oh, darn!" she swore, tears of frustration flowing.

"But anything else you might want, in exchange for invoking my dragon—"

"Nothing else," she said sadly.

"So you won't do it?"

"I won't," she agreed. "I named my price."

One I could not pay, as Boffo had foreseen, enjoying my coming frustration.

I left her weeping in the kitchen, feeling like a heel. At least now I knew.

Or did I? This sequence, too, was suspiciously convenient. Was it also part of the play?

Fiera's red line led me back to my suite just in time for Princess Rose to collect me. She was resplendent in a bejeweled evening gown, the loveliest woman I had ever seen. "You shouldn't have teased Mave like that," she reproved me. "She's a good girl."

What kind of communications did this castle have? Did everybody know everything the instant it happened? "I didn't realize I was teasing her," I said. "I just wanted to know about the dragon."

"I'm sure a little persuasion would change her mind about evoking it only in exchange for marriage. You don't need to be concerned about that."

"Persuasion?"

"Our local torture chamber is small but well equipped. I suspect that just the threat of having her nipples ripped out would be effective. No actual messy disfiguring torture would be required."

I stared at her, horrified. "You're not joking," I breathed.

"I never joke about serious matters. That dragon needs to be evoked."

This was the woman I loved? I couldn't tolerate it. "Don't. Even. Threaten," I said grimly.

She glanced at me, surprised. "Oh, I keep forgetting that you're not from the Realm. You have different sensitivities."

"True. Leave her alone."

She shrugged, leaving me my foibles. I was still learning things about the Realm, and not all of them were comfortable. If this was Rose's notion of dark humor, I was not amused.

We arrived at the banquet hall, where soft music played. It was well named; the banquet was sumptuous, with every kind of meat, vegetable, bread, and beverage. Mave herself served the pastries. "Thank you, sir," she murmured as she passed me. She knew!

Lovely scant-skirted dancing girls entertained us as we concluded the meal. "If you would like one of those for the night," Rose said, "Just point her out. She will be glad to oblige."

"Thanks, no," I demurred, suppressing another surge of cultural shock. Was she testing me for interest in any woman other than her?

"Or Mave. She would be happy to demonstrate what she could offer you in the marriage bed."

This was getting downright uncomfortable. "I'd rather have you."

"You would find me frustrating, as I must retain my virginity until marriage. Fortunately none of these are virgins."

I concluded that she was serious. "Thanks, I'll pass," I said.

"I shouldn't have kissed you yet. But you did insist on staring at me."

"My fault," I agreed. She might love me, as I loved her, but evidently had no problem with a man's incidental entertainments, quite apart from the callous requirements of royal union. Then I thought of something else. "You expect to have an arranged marriage."

Rose grimaced prettily. "Yes. I can get out of it only by marrying a man with better prospects." She glanced at me sidelong.

"Who is he?"

"Prince Obelisk, of a far kingdom, whose member is said to resemble his name. He is a warrior, quite skilled." Her mouth twitched. "And no, he is no more eager to do it than I am. He has his own girlfriend, apart from his harem. But it was arranged long ago by our families, and it would be perilous to go against it."

"Sorry to hear it," I said.

"It is the way. We do not rail against the inevitable."

It was late by the time it all finished. Rose escorted me to my room, but did not offer to join me there. Instead she kissed me chastely and departed. She was being true to her virginity.

I lay awake for some time, pondering imponderables, as I had before, with no better resolution. I loved Princess Rose, but was suspicious of her facility with my gun, considering that theoretically she had never seen such a weapon before. She was one tough-minded woman, as her threat about Mave showed. I had thought her to be shy, but that was evidently out of context; she was worldly in ways I was not, and in some aspects she was definitely not my type. Talk of arranged marriages—what about arranged love? I should have avoided it if humanly possible. So did we really love each other, or was she faking susceptibility to my stare? Was I psychologically overwhelmed by the presumed impact of her kiss? Would that impact fade in three days? My rational self advised me to give this time to sort itself out. I still didn't like the seeming coincidence of the ambushing bandit in the tree along a path no one should have known we would take, leading to Lord Mephisto's castle. Had Rose known he would be there?

And the dragon theme. Fiera was challenge enough, but that was hardly the half of it. They claimed I was a transformed dragon, but the confirmation of this had been way too easy. A dragon-evoker right here in the castle? My PI instinct railed against such coincidence. Certainly they wanted me to believe

I was the Dragon King, but was that really the case? Until this adventure I had never even believed in dragons.

And those assassinations, including my father, and the king (maybe)—those weren't all recent events. They had been going on for generations. There were some royals who did not seem to be in immediate peril, like Prince Obelisk. Why?

But mainly it was that I had no handle on reality here. It was like one of those newspaper cryptic quote puzzles, where every letter given was false, and the challenge was to figure out the correct letters and thus the original quote, like "No man is an island," etc. Only here I could not even be sure that everything was false. I would hate to think that Princess Rose was a lying schemer, or that my very presence here was a sham. I needed to find the key to make sense of this wild array of confusion.

The old king, Rose's adopted father, had had a good notion: get out of the picture for a while and see what the other players did. I wished I could do the same, but that wasn't feasible. I wished I could talk to him. Which made me wonder: why had Mephisto told me about the king's survival, instead of quietly finishing the job himself? And the question brought the answer: so that the gumshoe ignoramus from Earth would ferret out the hiding king, to question him—and thus lead the king's enemy right to him so he could be killed for good. *That* was the reason Mephisto had told me. What a colossal fool he figured me for! Almost successfully.

Then I suffered a blinding flash of understanding. The assassinations—they were not to eliminate prospective heirs to the throne, but to eliminate the hidden Dragon King! Because the Dragon would destroy any usurper, unless the Dragon were first eliminated himself. They did not know in whose body the Dragon hid, and were doubtless frustrated that they could never be sure the Dragon had been dealt with. Unless they located him, evoked him, and killed him. Then the throne would truly be open for usurping. So they needed to verify me as the Dragon King—and kill me. Because the Dragon had to be dead, and if I were not the Dragon I was of no use to them anyway and could be thrown away. By "them" I meant the anonymous assassin (who might or might not be Mephisto) and his minions, not Princess Rose and her loyal friends. But Rose might have been tricked into fetching me from Earth, and the assassin was watching closely. I was in the same danger as the king, for much the same reason.

I was in doubt whether I was the Dragon King, and there was a problem making the proof of that. The assassin was in doubt too, and wanted very much to know, one way or the other, so he could act. That was surely why Dubi and Rose had somehow been given the notion to bring me here: to find out. I would be best advised to see that this doubt remained indefinitely, or at least until I located the assassin and took him out. My life surely depended on it.

I drifted off into a troubled sleep, still not knowing my wisest course. What new horrors would the morrow bring?

CHAPTER THIRTEEN

I slept fitfully and awakened the next morning perhaps more tired than when I'd gone to sleep. I hated when that happened.

My guest suite was indeed fit for a king. Plush, four-poster bed. Ornate furniture. Thick animal hides. I used a nearby water basin to wash my face and a wash cloth to scrub my teeth. A clean detective is an effective detective. Although I knew very little of medieval architecture, this palace seemed surprisingly modern. I had no reason to believe the technical advances in the Realm coincided with advances on Earth; indeed, I knew so very little about the Realm. Were both worlds evolving at their own natural pace? Or was one influencing another? A lot to figure out, surely. Perhaps more than a common detective needed to worry about.

Especially a common detective who had been hired to find a killer.

I patted the pouch of gold in my front pocket. One way or another, I was getting this gold back to earth.

But first, a job to do.

That is, of course, if I wasn't being set up, which is what this was all beginning to feel like. If so, who was setting me up and why? What advantage would they gain by misleading me, an outsider? Yes, the clues had thus far fallen naturally (and easily) into place. But clues were clues, and facts were facts. Hard to argue with either.

"Except you don't have any real facts, do you, Mr. Detective?" I said to myself as I splashed more water on my face.

Indeed, only hearsay.

One of which was that the king was, in fact, still alive. I was here to find the king's assassin. If the king wasn't dead, well, my job would be complete. I could return home with my little pouch of gold—and another just like it, if Dubi and company upheld their end of the bargain—and try to forget any of this had ever happened.

Except, of course, if someone from the Realm had murdered my father.

If so, that would be another matter altogether.

For now, my goal was to look into Mephisto's allegations that the king had faked his death. After all, it was hard to investigate a murder if the victim was alive and well.

Once confirmed, this case was over. And if they wanted to hire me to find the would-be assassin, well, it would cost them more gold.

"One case at a time," I whispered, and headed down for breakfast.

I had buttered pastries on a wide balcony that overlooked much of what must have been the eastern Realm, if rising sun was any indicator. That was, of course, if the Realm was a parallel of earth as Dubi had suggested.

The princess was still asleep, which was just as well. When finished breaking my fast, as they called it here, I telepathically asked Fiera to summon Dubi for me. The invisible dragon, who was standing guard somewhere nearby, complied with a mental nod.

A moment later, the short wizard appeared at the balcony, blinking into the morning sun. I waved him over and he came hesitantly, looking warily over the ledge of the balcony.

"Are you okay?" I asked.

"Just not a fan of heights."

This surprised me, although I wasn't sure why. In his defense, the castle was situated high upon a craggy tor—and the balcony soared many hundreds of feet above the sprawling city far below.

"I see," I said. "Would you prefer we talk inside?"

"No, no. I'll be fine." He swallowed hard. "How is your investigation coming along, Detective Roan?"

"It's why I called you up," I said, although I regretted doing so now. "Lord Mephisto made a wild claim."

"As Lord Mephisto is wont to do," said the wizard, some humor returning to his voice.

"Be that as it may, he asserted that the king had not been assassinated. That the the king is very much alive."

The wizard blinked and some of the color returned to his cheeks. "Oh, really?"

"Yes. Further, he claims that you and the Matron would have knowledge of this. Is this true?"

"Is what true?"

"Is the king alive and do you have knowledge of this?"

"Lord Mephisto speaks with conviction for a man who has been banned from the castle. And for a man who, by all accounts, has been actively seeking to control the Realm."

I nodded and listened, noting with interest that the wizard had effectively evaded my question. I also watched his body language and listened closely to his tone of voice. Yes, some of the nuances were undoubtedly lost in translation, but what I was seeing was classic evasion. His eyes shifted. He lifted his hand to rub his chin. Averting the eyes and hiding the mouth were classic lying "tells."

"Perhaps," I said. "But does he speak the truth?"

Dubi turned away, looking out toward the rising sun. "The king is dead."

"Thank you, Dubi. I do not want to keep you up here longer than necessary."

He nodded sadly, took in some air, and left the balcony much faster than when he'd arrived.

When he was gone, I had Fiera summon the Matron. The dragon obliged, and shortly the stout woman who sported a permanent grimace came out onto the balcony.

"You summoned me, Sir Roan."

"Indeed," I said, still getting used to the formal title. Up until a day ago, the only 'sir' I heard was usually from an exasperated bill collector.

I asked the Matron to sit across from me, which she did. She declined a pastry and so I got to it, asking her what she knew of the possibility that the king had survived the attack.

"Nonsense," she said.

No hand covering her mouth. No looking away. In fact, she didn't move or even blink, as far as I could see.

"It seems that Lord Mephisto's claim should be explored."

"Explore if you must, but let me assure you that I saw the king's body."

"On the balcony," I said.

"Of course."

"Was he alone?"

"Yes."

"One arrow or two?"

"One."

"And this occurred at night?"

"Yes, I already told you all this."

I ignored her irritation. Investigators make a living by asking the same questions, to see if we get the same answers. "What were you doing just prior to hearing the king cry out?"

"I was making my rounds."

"What do your rounds consist of?"

"Checking on rooms, bathrooms, supplies."

"Did you check on the princess that night?"

"Yes."

"Before the king was attacked?"

"I think so, yes."

"You think so?"

"Yes, I'm sure of it. Just before."

"And she will attest to your claim?"

"I don't see why not. I thought I answered all of these questions be—"

"Do my questions make you uncomfortable?"

"Of course not."

"Very well," I said. "Was the king dead when you found him?"

"Yes."

"What position was he in?"

"Sitting up, propped against the door."

"The door into the bedroom?"

"Yes."

I visualized the king's balcony again. In fact, it wasn't very different from the one we were on now. The king could have taken the arrow...and stumbled back into the door, dying before he could go inside.

"Do you have any knowledge of the king faking his death?"

"None."

Is she telling the truth, Fiera?

Her mind is closed, Sir Roan.

Is it common for her mind to be closed?

I have never dipped into her mind before.

Then how would she know to close it?

She didn't, came Fiera's reply. *Until she was coached by Dubi just moments before you summoned her.*

Dubi?

I thought about that, and then thanked the Matron for her time. She nodded curtly and left.

I was alone in the castle, absently wandering the halls, feeling a bit lost but not worried about it. I always thought best when I was walking. I solved more cases by walking the streets of Los Angeles.

I came across more than one tapestry of the Dragon King. Standing guards, armed with short and long swords, dotted the palace and watched me suspiciously, but none stopped me. Apparently, I had been given permission to wander through the castle.

Dubi had seemed evasive. The Matron less so, although she just might be a better liar. Dubi had coached her to close her mind. Why? I thought about that as I walked. Obviously there was something there that he didn't want Fiera to ferret out. And, as the dragon admitted, it had never occurred to her dip into the Matron's mind before.

So what were Dubi and the Matron hiding?

The answer seemed obvious. If Lord Mephisto's hypothesis (and magic) was correct, they were hiding information regarding the death of the king.

I thought about this long and hard...and decided that I wouldn't know the truth until I truly found the king—and it looked like I wasn't going to get much help from the court wizard or the head of staff.

There was, however, one person who would be of help to me.

The princess herself.

———

I found her in her bedroom, sitting before a glass mirror and applying make-up.

"You have been very active this morning, according to Fiera," she said, glancing at me in the mirror. I stood behind her, marveling at the smoothness of her shoulders, the perfect sweep of her slender neck, the thickness of her fair hair. Yeah, that love spell had done a number on me. The perfection of her neck? Never had such a thought occurred to me...and yet...her neck looked so very perfect. And so very kissable.

I somehow managed to control myself. "You didn't hire me to sleep."

She nodded, running a comb slowly through her lustrous hair. "Am I still a suspect to my own father's murder? I thought you confirmed my innocence?"

"I had, but I'm here to follow up on the possibility that your father might—"

"Still be alive? Oh, rubbish!" said Rose, slamming her comb down. "Lord Mephisto is clearly lying."

"What does he gain by lying?"

"Who knows? Maybe to deflect blame."

"And why wait twenty or so years to exact his revenge?"

"You will have to ask him that."

"I did," I said evenly. "And he assured me that he did not kill the king. I believe him."

"He is a liar and you are a fool to believe him."

"He is also your father."

"My real father was murdered, and Lord Mephisto is going to pay."

She resumed brushing her hair, and I decided to approach this from another angle, an angle that had occurred to me while walking the castle passageways. "Did your father have a fear of heights?"

She nodded almost instantly. "Deathly."

"Were your father and Dubi good friends?"

She frowned and glanced at me in the mirror. "Of course. Dubi is the royal wizard, trusted for decades."

"Did he actually say he trusted Dubi?"

"On many occasions. We all do."

I paused before asking my next question, then plunged forward. "Did you ever, in fact, see your father and Dubi together?"

She stopped brushing again. "What do you mean?"

"Did you ever see your father and the wizard together in the same room, side by side?"

"Of course. What a ridiculous—"

"Think back," I urged.

"Of course..." she began, but then closed her mouth. She opened it to speak again, but then promptly closed it again. Next, the brush clattered to the floor. "What are you implying?"

Fiera, I said, *send for Dubi.*

I already have, Sir Roan.

A moment later, the door to the bedroom suite opened and Dubi strode in.

"Two summons in one morning," said the wizard jovially enough. "To what do I owe the pleasure?"

"Dubi," said Princess Rose, rising. "Sir Roan might need some medical aid."

"Oh?" said the wizard, raising a bushy eyebrow. "What ails you, detective?"

"He's obviously suffered a head injury because he's not thinking straight. Sir Roan thinks that you are the king."

The wizard's eyes widened briefly, and he turned his back to us and faced the open balcony door.

"Tell him he's crazy, Dubi," she said. I heard the tremble in her voice, and didn't blame her. "Please."

"I can't tell him that," said the wizard, turning. "Because he's not."

Princess Rose gasped. I might have gasped, too. It was one thing to have a hunch, but quite another to be right.

It was then that the princess fainted.

She might have hit the floor hard if not for a wispy, billowy cushion appearing beneath her. She landed softly, where she lay unharmed, and quite unconscious. I went immediately to her side and checked her vitals. She was breathing, just out cold.

Dubi swept to her side as well, and passed a hand just over her body. He patted her cheek tenderly, then stood. "She will be fine," said Dubi. "I'm afraid she's suffered one too many shocks over the past few days."

I picked her up carefully and laid her on the bed. "Two fathers," I said. "In two days."

"Enough to make any one faint." He looked at me. "How did you know?" In that moment, he shimmered and appeared before me as another man entirely. A handsome man, actually. A man who looked strikingly like my father.

The thought nearly overwhelmed me. He was, of course, my grandfather. My father's father.

I'm going crazy, I thought. In fact, I suddenly felt lightheaded. Dubi guided me to a nearby stool. "Easy, old boy," he said.

He stood over me while I collected my thoughts. Finally, I said, "You share a fear of heights."

"Very good," he said. "But many have such a fear. Surely there was more to lead you to believe I was the king."

"That, and you and the king were never in the same room. Undoubtedly you worked double time concealing your identity as Dubi."

"It was a challenge and oft-times I confused the roles."

"But why a wizard?" I asked.

The handsome older man regarded me with my father's eyes. "I was a king by birth, but a wizard by choice."

"I don't understand."

"As you are aware, royalty have the potential for magic. The potential within me was great. Too great for me to ignore."

"And so you created Dubi the Magician."

"He has served me well. I can watch over my kingdom and watch over my daughter."

I stood and paced before the bed where the princess still lay resting. "But why summon me from earth?" I asked. "If it was all a charade?"

"Oh, it wasn't as much of a charade as you might think, Detective. My guards and I had been well aware that there was a plot afoot to assassinate me. However, try as we might, we were unable to locate the source of the attack."

"Lord Mephisto?"

"Is harmless. Yes, he bore a grudge against me for stealing his girlfriend—Rose's mother, in fact. But no one loved her more than I, although my time with her was comparatively brief. No, Lord Mephisto does not have it in him for treason against his country and king."

"Then who?"

"It is why I brought you here, Detective Roan. Or, should I say, one of the reasons."

"I don't understand."

"There is a great army amassing in the north. Bigger than, I'm afraid, we can defend against."

We were silent. Princess Rose made a small sound in her sleep. She stirred slightly. She would be, I suspected, awakening soon. "You need the Dragon King," I said after a while.

"Now more than ever."

CHAPTER FOURTEEN

Princess Rose opened her eyes and found herself in disarray. Her hair was messed up, her full bodice was slightly askew, and her pleated skirt was flopped up over her lovely knees. She spied me watching. "Do you see anything interesting, Sir Roan?" she inquired archly.

"Absolutely fascinating, and I can't wait to get my hands on it," I said candidly. "But at the moment I am more concerned with the state of your outlook. You fainted when you learned that your father survives. Can you accept it now?"

"I can," she said. "Beneath this frilly exterior there lies a moderately smart realist. But it was a shock."

I looked at Dubi. I knew him now for the king, but I still thought of him as the wizard. "One thing bothers me. Your secret has now been exposed. It seems that everyone in this castle knows about the latest gossip almost before it happens. You are surely in danger again."

"I surely am," Dubi agreed. "But that army to the north is virtually ready to strike, so my guiding hand is needed here. Rose is not versed in military defense. I had hoped to cause the assassin to reveal himself, but now perforce I must govern."

"And there is still an assassin," I said. "Even if you're not dead. So my job continues."

"I'm an absolute mess, and confused by recent revelations," Rose said. "So if you worthy men will get out of my room, I will put myself in order." She lifted her legs and swung them off the bed, providing me with a near-paralyzing flash, as she surely realized.

"Even as a confused mess, you remain prettier than any other woman I know," I said honestly.

"You don't count. I kissed you."

"Touche," I agreed.

"Perhaps we should adjourn to the balcony," Dubi said.

I stifled a double-take. He wanted to go out where his fear of heights would constrict him? There had to be excellent reason. "As you wish."

Dubi reverted to his familiar Wizard form as we departed the bedroom.

"There is something on your mind?" I asked when we reached the balcony.

"It's about the castle network. You have noted how news gets rapidly about, but you don't seem to understand precisely how."

"That's true." I realized now that this was a bad gap in my information.

"It is a telepathic ambiance that can develop in well-used castles. They seem to tune in on their inhabitants, sharing their thoughts as it were, or at least their voices. Anything you say can be overheard by other parties who are interested enough to pay close attention. It is especially acute when the listener is the subject of a dialogue."

That explained a lot. "So when I talked to Mave, Rose overheard. And when I talked to Rose, Mave heard."

"Exactly. Both are quite taken with you, so tend to listen in on your dialogues with the other. But they are not the only ones interested in you. As a newcomer, and an investigator, and perhaps royal, and possibly even the Dragon King, you are the current main person of interest."

"But that means that this conversation is being heard," I said. "We have no secrets."

"Not so. Did it occur to you to wonder why I chose to have my death out here, despite my nervousness about the exposure?"

Then I caught on. "Because you needed privacy! Otherwise everyone would know it was fake."

"Exactly."

"And that is why we are talking here now. So that we can't be overheard by the castle. You must have something really important to tell me."

"Not so," he repeated.

For a moment I was baffled. "Not?"

"It is to prevent you from saying anything that might prejudice your mission."

I assimilated that. "Sir, I wish I could tell you I had a lead on the assassin, but I don't."

"But you will find that lead. I have observed you at work. You have the mind for it."

"I hope you're right. But it seems I can't investigate anyone here without everyone knowing. That crimps my style."

"Not necessarily. You can make the network work for you."

"I can?"

"Allow me to demonstrate. We shall reenter the castle. Focus on listening for references to yourself. Do not speak aloud."

"I will do that," I agreed dubiously.

We went back inside. I stood there beside Dubi, listening. And I started to hear voices, first whisper-faint, then as it attuned, louder and clearer.

'Don't touch that sweetbread. It is reserved for Sir Roan.'

'Ellie, you will clean Sir Roan's room today.' 'Yes ma'am.' 'Say, Ellie, wouldn't it be funny if you ripped off the sheets with your usual carelessness, and he was still in the bed! He sleeps naked, you know.' 'I'd be so embarrassed!' 'You'd have to take off your own clothes and jump in with him!' 'No!' 'You're blushing, Ellie.'

There was more, but I'd had enough. I could indeed do some research this way, without ever leaving my room. Unless shy Ellie came. I wondered what she looked like. I also wondered how they knew I slept naked. Maybe the last cleanup maid had not found any pajamas with the sheets.

We returned to the balcony. "This is amazing. Thank you, sir, for acquainting me with it. I will be very careful about anything I say within the castle."

"Much of interest can be overheard," Dubi said. "It is a prime pastime among the servants, and perhaps the royals too. Needless to say, illicit sexual liaisons are performed in utter silence, unless the participants don't mind advertising. Any maid who got in bed with you would want to advertise."

"Thanks for the warning."

"You are free to do what you wish at night, but Rose will know."

I appreciated that warning too. "She told me I could have any dancer for the night. She did not seem jealous."

"Yes, of course. Rose knows better than to try to restrict a man's pleasures. But do not say anything private during such a liaison."

"Such as my thoughts about the identity of the assassin?"

"Exactly. Some men can become careless at such times."

Right on. "Thank you again, sir. I will not be careless."

"I did not mean to suggest that you would be." He was the soul of diplomacy. The more I got to know the king, the better I liked him. "Are there any other private matters you wish to mention before we go public again?" He glanced nervously at the ledge, and I realized that he was making a sacrifice to educate me privately.

"Um, how soon do you think that army to the north will attack?" I asked.

"It can occur at any moment. It has been massing for the past month."

"Exactly how could the Dragon King deal with it?"

"That we do not know. Only that it will be effective."

"Assuming, of course, that I am that Dragon. I have no certainty of that."

"We sincerely hope that you are the Dragon, because otherwise we are lost."

"I hope so too," I said humbly.

"One more caution: a dragon, when first evoked, is not fully functional at the outset. Like a butterfly emerging from a cocoon, it requires time to consolidate its various powers. The Dragon King has been quiescent for a considerable period. So you will want to do it in as much privacy as you can manage."

"And the assassin will be watching," I added. "In or outside the castle. Ready to strike the moment he is sure of the Dragon's identity. Because he can't afford to let the Dragon achieve those powers."

Dubi nodded soberly. "You have a marvelous grasp of the situation."

And that's when I told him my plan. Dubi listened quietly, occasionally raising his eyebrows and nodding. When I was finished, he said, "A marvelous plan, Sir Roan. I will need only a little time on my end. See me an hour before noon tomorrow, and we shall put your plan into motion. Now I will leave you to your own devices. I have a kingdom to run."

He certainly did, and I sincerely appreciated the time he had taken with me.

What was I to do now? Assuming I was the Dragon King—which I feared was an uncomfortably long shot—I could not be safely invoked without considerably more privacy than this castle offered. I would not be safe away from the castle either, unless I could spirit Mave away to Lord Mephisto's castle to do the deed. That threatened to be more complicated than I could manage. What I really needed to do was locate and eliminate the anonymous assassin. Then the rest should fall into place reasonably readily.

I went to my room and lay down to think. And wouldn't you know it, that was when the chamber maid came to clean it up. I sat up as she entered, and she really was pretty. "Ellie, I presume?"

"Oh!" she said, and wavered on her feet as if about to faint.

I hurried to stabilize her. "I knew you were coming," I said. "I couldn't resist teasing you. I'll get out of here and let you work in peace."

"Thank you sir," she said faintly.

I departed the room and headed for the kitchen to pick up my sweetbread. The castle personnel had zeroed in on my tastes with telepathic speed. Too bad I couldn't zero in similarly on the assassin.

Then I felt it coming like a storm on the horizon. It was an idea how to locate the assassin. I didn't have it yet, but it was on the way. I opened my mind to it—and it fizzed out. All I could think of was how I had learned to play chess as a kid, and a more experienced player had got me four times in succession with the Fool's Mate. What a humiliation! Later I spied in a magazine a counter trap to reverse the case when someone tried the Fool's Mate, but I never got to use it. Ever thus, like the perfect retort to an insult. Now if I could just reverse the case with the assassin…

Then it hit me. That was the key! To lay myself open for the assassin, then nab him when he struck. He'd never suspect a counter-trap.

I went to Princess Rose's room and knocked on her door. She opened it, standing there fully prettied up. I wished I could enfold her, but I had a different agenda at the moment. "I have a plan," I said.

She let me in. "You can't have my virginity until marriage."

I liked her humor. "Not that plan. It's to get Mave to evoke my dragon. I'll need to spend the night with her. One night should do it."

"You're going to Stare her!" she exclaimed admiringly.

I frowned in mock distaste. "That would be unfair."

"All's fair in love and war, especially when they merge."

"Obviously all I really want from her is sex. I'll have to offer her a face-saving deal, like being First Concubine after I marry you, and siring a Royal Bastard. It's not much, but I think it is doable."

"I like the way your devious mind works. By morning you'll have her eating out of your hand, or whatever." Her gaze flicked down to my belt or thereabouts. "She'll do anything you want."

"And what I want is for her to evoke my dragon at noon tomorrow. In front of everyone in the castle, so that the assassin won't dare to strike."

She clapped her hands in girlish glee. "We'll all be there."

I frowned. "Aren't you even a little bit jealous?"

"Oh, yes. I'll envy her that night. But it's a chore you have to do."

Some chore. I let it pass, just as she had let my mention of marriage pass. "I'm going to get some daytime sleep. I want to be alert for the chore."

"By all means." She stepped forward and delivered one of her chaste kisses. "I still think torture might be a safer bet, but we'll play it your way. We need that dragon."

I returned to my room. Ellie was just finishing up. "That looks great," I said.

"Thank you, sir," she simpered.

"Tell Mave I want her with me tonight."

She froze briefly, then recovered. "I will, sir."

I realized that I had been needlessly cruel. "Your turn will come, Ellie. I met her before I met you, so she's ahead in line. Protocol."

She blushed scarlet and departed, pleased.

I lay down on the freshly made bed. I did need rest and sleep, because I suspected it was going to be a difficult night, albeit not for the reason the gossip listeners expected.

The day passed routinely, though I was conscious of the attention of the staff. They all knew that I wanted raw sex, and that Mave wanted a commitment, and were even placing bets (I did a snooping listen) on the outcome. Would I persuade her to evoke my dragon without marriage, or would her phenomenal sex appeal win me over? Or would it be a draw: no marriage, no Dragon?

Mave arrived promptly as I turned in for the night. She was breathtakingly beautiful in a harem girl outfit, and scented with what I suspected was an erotic perfume. "I know we should spend some token time getting to know each other better," I told her. "But I can't wait. Join me in the shower."

She disrobed in something like half a second and joined me in the shower without protest. Evidently she had some experience with kinky male tastes. I put my arms around her in the blasting water and whispered in her ear. Her jaw dropped, then she nodded. She would play along, at least for now.

"I'd love to have at you," I whispered. "As you can see from the arousal of my body. But this is business. There is an army massing on the kingdom's north border, and soon it will invade and wipe us out. Only the Dragon King can stop it. I need you to evoke it now, so that it has the night to consolidate and come into its proper power. Otherwise the assassin will destroy it at the outset, tomorrow at noon, and all will be lost. I appeal to your patriotism. You know the terms I proffer, and I will honor them and be truly grateful for your help. Without you I can't do it."

She turned her face and whispered her response in my ear. "The princess's kisses don't last more than a few days. Then you won't be her love slave any more. If something happens to mess up your marriage with her, will you marry me instead?"

"Provided that nothing bad happens to the princess, so that it is her choice to void the marriage, then yes, I will marry you. But I see little likelihood of that happening."

"Then I will be First Concubine with a Royal Bastard," she said. "It is a fair deal, and we will save the kingdom."

"Oh, thank you!" I said, hugely grateful. I held her and kissed her passionately.

"No sex at this time," she said regretfully. "You will need that energy to fill out the dragon." Then she put her hands on my head and exerted her power.

It was magnificent. Maybe our nakedness and emotion contributed, or maybe it was simply the hot water, but I felt a massive arousal in my body and mind. The Dragon was stirring, preparing to come out.

And did it ever. I swelled into a mass of flesh too big for the shower. My coils filled the bathroom, my tail extending into the bedroom. My head became a toothy giant, my arms and legs scaly, my digits clawed. Still she stayed with me, her hands on my head, keeping the evocation going. She knew what she was doing.

Then I was complete, filling all available space, coiled three layers deep. But I was weak, hardly able to support my own enormous weight.

"It will take a while for your strength to come," she said. "But you should be able to transform back to human shape now."

I concentrated, and it worked. I resumed my human form. But I was abysmally weak.

Mave turned off the shower and led me to the bed. She laid me down on it, then joined me, putting her hands back on my head. I felt the healing power, and knew that the conversion was still happening, this time internally. Without her strength I would have been completely lost. She was right about skipping the sex; I needed every bit of that energy for the evocation.

Then she did something that surprised and pleased me immeasurably: she faked sex. I was too washed out to do it, but didn't need to. "What, so soon again?" she asked with seeming surprise. "After all those times in the shower? Well, I'm game if you can do it." She was briefly silent, then she started moaning as if in ascending pleasure, culminating in an urgent simulated climax. "Oh, you did," she said. "What a performance!" The performance, of course, was hers; she was a born actress.

Meanwhile she kept her hands on my head, channeling the evocation, and I felt the strength rising as my inner organs fell into place. My muscles were hardening, and my belly was generating literal fire. But that was only part of it. I was discovering that the Dragon King was more mental than physical, and that alien mind had power I had never dreamed of. Telepathy, of course, but also teleportation, clairvoyance, and other abilities that were fearsome in their potential. Destroy an army? This mind could make that army lie down and die without fighting, or flee in terror from a mouse. Truly, I was the Dragon King, and this dragon was the salvation of the kingdom.

"Again?" Mave asked. "I don't know whether I can—oooh, do that again!" And she went into another slow simulation.

Then later in the night she said something else. "And you didn't even Stare me. You are conquering me without the Stare." That was technically true, but she was making it sound far more significant.

Finally I spoke, partly to be sure I could do it. "It is my logic I want you to heed."

"That, too," she sighed ecstatically. "Sir Roan, you have won me. I have never had a night like this. I will perform the evocation at noon, as you direct."

As morning came I knew the dragon was as yet incomplete, but so great was its potential that even this partial fulfillment was more than I had seen in Fiera, and my magic was more than I had seen in the Wizard. I was ready to take on any likely assassin. Now all I needed was for that assassin to attack me at noon, thinking me vulnerable, thus betraying his identity at last.

As dawn cracked the sky, Mave went into one more enactment, panting her desperate fulfillment. "Oh Sir Roan!" she gasped. "It will take me weeks to recover from the force of your plumbing, and years to stop dreaming of it!" Then she got up and limped away.

I loved Princess Rose, but now I also loved Mave. What a woman!

I dropped off to sleep at last, knowing the dragon strength was still growing. Mave had gotten it fairly started, and now it could continue on its own.

An hour before noon, I awoke. No one had disturbed me. Mave must have told them to stay clear, bless her again. I changed smoothly into dragon form, then back to human. I was ready.

I first went down and met with Dubi. Once finished, I went to the central courtyard. I had said aloud that I thought I would be protected because I would be evoked in a public place with many spectators. That was deliberately naïve. I knew the assassin would strike regardless, contemptuous of all except the weak nascent Dragon. A crowd had gathered for the event. Mave was there, looking slightly disheveled as if unable to recover completely from her sexual workout. Marvelous!

Wordlessly I stepped out with her, the princess, Dubi and a handful of heavily armed guards. On with the show!

CHAPTER FIFTEEN

It was a glorious day for an evocation, words that I never thought I would say. Or think. But here I was, with the sun shining high above, standing within a castle courtyard, a heaving, excited crowd waiting for me to transform into, of all things, a savior dragon.

Life is weird, I thought, as I looked out over the growing crowd. Word had gotten out that the Dragon King would be making his first public appearance. I likened this to be similar the Second Coming in my own world. Except, of course, I was no son of God.

Just a dragon, apparently. I shook my head at the craziness of it all. Last week I was following cheating spouses. Today I was the Dragon King.

Maybe, I thought. But I was still hired to do a job. To find the assassin. Yes, the king wasn't dead. But my father was dead. And his death, I was certain, was linked to all of this.

They killed him, I suspected, because they thought he had been the Dragon King. They were wrong, of course. The dubious honor fell to me.

Undoubtedly, the assassin had realized his or her error. The Dragon King hadn't been the king himself, nor my father—both of whom the assassin had killed, or so he or she thought in the case of the king.

Now, of course, the assassin was after me.

Yes, I thought, let the games begin.

I kept my mind closed from the telepathic dragon, just as I had commanded Mave to do. No one must know the plan. Rose

108

was by my side, smiling. Dubi was nearby as well, hands behind his back, looking uncomfortable. Guards stood guard everywhere, keeping the rowdy crowd back. But it wasn't the crowd I feared.

No. It was one lone assassin.

He—or she—was out there somewhere, biding their time, waiting to put an arrow in me.

Princess Rose reached out and squeezed my hand. I squeezed back. She smiled at me and frowned a little. I quickly released her hand, lest she become suspicious and blow my cover.

Now Mave reached up and put her hands on my head. My heart raced. For the first time, I felt nervous. What if I had miscalculated? What if the assassin wasn't here?

He had to be. Or *she* had to be. My every instinct told me he or she would be. The assassin would stop the evocation at all costs. He or she would stop the Dragon King's manifestation. Something would happen. Something would happen now, before the evocation. I was sure of it.

The crowd cheered, heaved, a sea of excited humanity. My heart raced, too. I felt Mave's warm hands on my head. Time seemed to stop. I held my breath.

"Wait!" shouted a voice.

I turned my head at the voice. A familiar voice. It had come, of course, from Princess Rose herself. She was pointing a crossbow at my chest.

"Rose," I said, but that's as far as I got.

The bolt was loosed, plunging deep into my heart. The pain was intense, but mercifully brief, and I crumpled to the ground, one hand on the bolt, one hand reaching for the princess. I looked up for a moment or two. I looked deep into Rose's eyes. She was not the Rose I knew and loved. She was hard, cold, bitter. Indeed, she nearly looked like another persona altogether.

And then my heart collapsed, and my eyes shut, and I breathed my last.

The courtyard was thrown into pandemonium.

I watched all of this from above, as spirits are wont to do. The guards, confused, were ordered by Dubi to fetch the princess, which they dutifully did. Guards, princess, Mave, Dubi and my lifeless body were all swept into the castle throne room, where the massive doors were thrown shut and sealed.

I drifted into the court room, as well, high above, watching all.

Outside, the crowd was in a wild panic, and I didn't blame them. Their Dragon King had been killed before their eyes. Undoubtedly they knew that an army was waiting in the north, an army that would now descend upon them, perhaps killing all.

Yes, I had surely flushed out the killer, but I had not expected it to be my sweet Rose, whose love spell still clung to my dead heart.

Princess Rose was dragged through the courtroom, where she was deposited unceremoniously at the feet of Dubi the magician, the king, her father. Thus far, only she and myself, and perhaps Matron, knew of Dubi's disguise. Still, Dubi could not hide the disappointment and regret in his voice.

"Why, Rose?" he asked, his voice full of anguish. "Why did you do it?"

She said nothing, not at first. I watched from above, curious.

"What did you hope to gain, my daughter?" he asked, and at that he transformed into the king. The guards gasped. One or two stumbled back. The king held up his hands. "Be still, my guards. Yes, your king is alive and well. All will be explained soon enough. For now, we have a traitor of the Realm to contend with. My own daughter."

Outside, the crowd still shouted. I might have smelled smoke. They were getting rowdy.

The king stood over his daughter, his face clouded with disappoint, confusion and shame. "So it was you? It was you who put an arrow in my heart. Have I not been good to you?"

Still, Rose did not speak. She was trembling now. A great shadow swept past the throne room's window. Fiera. She was circling the castle, and would, I knew, do all she could to come to the princess's aid. I watched as Mave slipped out of the room, and up a side flight of stairs. Good idea. Things were about to get very ugly, I suspected.

"What do you have to say for yourself, my daughter?" demanded the king.

"Do not be too hard on her, my old friend," said a deep voice from the shadows.

Like everyone else in the throne room, I snapped my head around. It was Lord Mephisto, of course. Two of the guards, recognizing him, instantly loosed two bolts in his direction. Mephisto casually waved his hand, and the projectiles clattered harmlessly to the floor.

The flying dragon, I realized, hadn't been so much as circling the castle, watching over her mistress, as depositing Lord Mephisto here, in the castle, thus bypassing the magical wards that kept the enemy away.

"And why shouldn't I be hard on my traitor daughter?" asked the king. He strode carefully out into the throne room. Guards all trained their weapons on the intruder wizard, but all present knew such weapons would have little impact.

Mephisto now stood before the king in the center of the throne room. Princess Rose watched from the far end, still on her hands and knees. She was weeping. Most importantly, the coldness in her eyes was gone. The Rose I knew had returned.

From the rafter high above, I finally spoke. "Your daughter was under a spell, my liege. As she had been for some time. Perhaps ever since her father—her real father, Lord Mephisto— first visited her in the orphanage."

All heads looked up, including Rose, who gasped. It was she who spoke first. "Sir Roan? You are not dead?"

The king grinned. He had been, of course, privy to my ruse, since it had been one of his magic dolls that had been cast into my likeness. And not just my likeness. With the king's considerable magic I had been able to animate the doll from afar. I could feel what it felt. Hear what it heard. It was a remarkable feat of magic that had exhausted the king, and would only last a short time.

Lord Mephisto, no fool, caught on instantly. "A fake, of course. Very clever, my king."

"Your plan to kill off the Dragon King has failed, Mephisto," said the king. "Give up now or die."

Rose's real father grinned. The guards trained their weapons on him. The shadow of the dragon passed by the window again. It was circling the castle.

"You would like that, my liege," said Lord Mephisto. "You would like having me give up so readily, when I have worked so hard to steal all that you love, just as you stole all that I loved."

The king said nothing, only regarded the tall man before him sadly. Rose was now on her feet. She was looking up at me. I saw the pain in her eyes, the sorrow. I winked at her. Mave appeared on the upstairs rafters, panting slightly, and looking beautiful. Yes, she had definitely stolen some of my heart last night.

"There is an army amassing in the north," said Mephisto. "An army that I have painstakingly aligned with—"

"The Shadow Stealers," said the king, nodding. Both men were now circling each other. "You sold your soul and kingdom. For what? Petty revenge?"

"Much more than that, my liege," said Mephisto, and with that a great crack of lightning erupted from the man's hand. "They have taught me the dark arts, as you can see. They only asked for one thing in return."

"Destroy the Dragon King," said the king.

Mephisto grinned wickedly and looked up at me. "And I see that I have failed, which is a problem."

"Because you have already informed the Shadow Stealers that the Dragon King is dead."

"You are smarter than you look, my liege. Now, I must finish the job!"

And as he spoke these words, something exploded through the Throne Room's stained-glass windows. It was the dragon, Fiera, and she was coming straight for me.

It was then that I realized the dragon had never been fully free of Mephisto's command. I had been fooled.

I turned to Mave. "Invoke the dragon. Hurry!"

Chapter Sixteen

Mave reached precariously for me on the rafter, ready to put on the show. She knew I was already the Dragon King and didn't need her help at this point, but she was adept at playing the role I had assigned her.

Too late. Fiera reached me first, her jaws opening wide to take me in. Trapped on the rafter, I could not escape her. She would hold me with her teeth, and breathe out just enough fire to roast me without further harming the castle furnishings. Obviously Mephisto did not want the castle damaged more than necessary, as he expected to govern it, with Rose as his puppet princess.

I did not even try. I let the dragon's teeth close on my flesh. There they halted, encountering my invulnerable skin. She could not hurt me. Her eyes widened in amazement.

You have the power already! she thought.

"Indeed," I answered her verbally. "You are in my power. If you doubt it, try to open your mouth."

She tried, but it was locked in place. She had been trapped by her own eagerness to dispatch me. *I am caught,* she confessed.

"Now yield to me."

I serve another, she thought with regret.

I drew my gun. "Now I could plug you through the brain," I said conversationally. "But you have been helpful to me in the past, and I'd like to have your loyalty in the future. Yield to me now, quietly, and I will spare you."

I cannot. Now she was hurting, and aspects of her pain were leaking out telepathically. The geis on her was too great. She was magically bound by a power beyond that of any ordinary dragon.

I considered briefly. I didn't want to kill her; Rose would be saddened. "Then I must do it the hard way," I said with my own regret. And without pause I blasted her with my Dragon King powered telepathy, which was a magnitude greater than hers. It bashed away her mental defense like straw and ripped open her mind. In seconds she would die if I did not ease off.

Then I paused. Her mind was laid out before me like the entrails of a split-open carcass and I saw something that amazed me. I grasped it instantly, though it covered years.

The attack on my father had not been by a person emulating Princess Rose. It had been by Rose herself, under the same spell that had just caused her to shoot my doll emulation. She was in the thrall not merely of Lord Mephisto, but of the sinister mind of the ruler of the Shadow Stealers that governed him. The deal Mephisto had made with the Shadow King was no recent thing; it dated back decades, and now at last was coming to its dreadful fruition.

But it was more than that. The princess, posing as a distressed client, took my father's own gun from the desk drawer and fired it at him. He had never anticipated such a thing from a seemingly innocent and lovely young woman. Her aim was imperfect (that would change thereafter) and the bullet did not kill him; it lodged in his ribcage. But the wound was enough to fell him, and he dropped to the floor, bleeding copiously. Her job done, the princess quickly departed, with no memory of the event.

But it did not end there. Mephisto appeared, carrying what I recognized as one of the king's life sized voodoo dolls. It was made in the image of my father, except that it bore no bullet wound; it looked as if it had been mysteriously poisoned, or perhaps even had died naturally. Mephisto lifted my father's body telekinetically, making it float, and laid the doll in its place as the blood evaporated. Then he and the body vanished.

Still it did not end. Fiera knew, and therefore so did I, now, that my father was transported to the Northern Kingdom of the Realm, where he was magically healed. He was told that the princess was on the way to usurping the throne of the Middle Kingdom (no relation to any ancient Chinese empire on Earth) and would in due course murder her adopted father and take over. Roan Quigley Senior, my father, had been targeted because he was the bastard son of the king, in line to inherit the throne if no fully legitimate heir was available. Now he was needed to take back the Middle Kingdom when the evil princess finally made her move. To that end he trained as a leader, and came to command a great northern army. He could not strike as long as the legitimate king was in place, but when the treacherous adopted princess took over, it would be time. That was projected to be about a month from now.

To ensure victory, Mephisto had enlisted the aid of the Shadow Stealers. These were largely invisible, unknowable entities who dwelt in an alternate dimension. They had no physical presence, but could take over the bodies of physical folk by first inhabiting their shadows, then gradually infiltrating the body. This took time, and was not done indiscriminately, because if the subject caught on too soon he could readily banish the intruder with a simple exorcism spell. Princess Rose's shadow had been occupied when she was but a child. She was a creature of the Shadow Stealers, but did not know it, and normally they left her to her own devices. So she was herself except when there was an emergency; then she was a foreign agent with deadly intentions, who could, I realized, heartlessly utilize torture or brutally kill. Contrary to what my father was told, the real Rose was not a schemer and not the enemy, and she had not killed anyone of her own volition. She, like Fiera, was governed as convenient by the Shadow Stealers.

Mephisto intended to put Rose in power, as the puppet. But Mephisto himself was a puppet of his supposed allies, the Shadow Stealers. It was a devious, decades-long project. Fiera knew all about it, but could not tell anyone, though she had her misgivings. Her job was to protect the physical princess, not the mental one, and at times that really griped her.

Then the king, suspecting something, had made a genius ploy and faked his own death. That had prompted immediate action, and the princess had come to collect the next likely heir, me. Because my father had turned out not to be the Dragon King, I was, by default, the best remaining prospect. The true target being the Dragon King, as I had surmised, because nothing less could stop the Shadow King from taking over, now that his time had come.

All this I read in an instant, while the ongoing action seemed to freeze around us. Now it was time to act. I banished the Shadow presence from Fiera's mind with a flick of my will, and put her back together. "Now you serve me," I told her with certainty. "Go guard the princess."

But she remains in thrall to the Shadow.

"Don't tell her you know." I could banish her Shadow, but at the moment I had a more dangerous enemy to deal with, and delay might be costly.

She reoriented and glided down to join Princess Rose. I saw that Boffo Bandit had made his way to her also. She would be well protected.

Mave had paused. "They know you're the Dragon King already," she said. She had a certain sense about such things, unsurprisingly.

"That's right. No need to continue our act. I do appreciate your readiness, however. Our deal remains: First Concubine, Royal Bastard. Climb back down to the floor."

She looked down. "I'm not sure I can." I knew her problem: she had climbed up in a fit of urgency to help me. Climbing down was another matter.

I smiled. "I will help you. Relax." I reached out and lifted her with my mind, floating her gently down to the floor. I saw several men looking up, admiring her shapely legs under the flaring skirt as she descended.

"Thank you, sir," Mave called as she landed. Then she glared around at the peeking men who had taken advantage of her situation.

Meanwhile, I oriented on Mephisto. I took hold of his mind and banished the Shadow presence there, as I had with Fiera. In the process I saw that he had in effect framed himself, planting the clues we had followed to identify him as a leading suspect. He had wanted to be suspected, then vindicated as I saw the shallowness of the evidence. Nice counter-intelligence, really.

He staggered, dazed. "What have I done!" He should be all right, freed of the Shadow.

I considered things as I sat on the rafter. I had set the immediate situation mostly to rights. But yet again, it seemed too easy. What was I missing? Things had worked out before because the enemy presence had been subtly manipulating them, shaping up the larger situation for the masked takeover. We had all been chess pieces playing into the Fool's Mate. The real enemy remained: the Shadow Stealers. They had no tangible presence, only their minions when they occupied human beings. How could I address them? My job was not finished until I did.

Be not concerned, reptile. I am here. You have done more than enough mischief.

I heard him in my mind, but saw nothing. Only maybe the faintest flicker of warmth in the air. It was the Shadow King.

I see you tricked my minions by evoking half a day ahead of your schedule, just as the king did by pretending death. But I am beyond such trickery. You may have power over mortal creatures, but it will be some time before you are my equal.

I felt the awesome power of his mind, and knew immediately that I was over-matched. He was correct: maybe in a few more hours I might be able to fight him, but at present I could not.

My ploy had sufficed to defeat the mortal entities I had known about, but this was an immortal with centuries of experience.

The Shadow King had arranged to evoke the Dragon King so he could finally identify and destroy him. I, not understanding the full nature of the trap, had walked right into it. That was likely not only to end my life, but to hurt my professional pride. I did not much like being played for a fool.

He did not mind speak again. Instead he laid siege to my mind, enclosing it in a sphere of dreadful dissolution. I defended myself, of course, fending him off, but that could only slow, not halt, the incursion. He would squeeze me like a ball of snow, leaving only a dribble of melt-water.

I bolted, escaping his deadly clutch. But he followed, playing with me like a cat with a mouse, knowing he could finish me at his whim. His emotions were obscure, because he was not human, but I knew he was enjoying this. He did not want it to be over too soon.

What could I do? It had never occurred to me that I would be the victim, once I became the Dragon King. Now I had to prevail, or die, and the fate of the kingdom, indeed, of the Realm, would follow mine. Without the Dragon King to defend it, the mortal scheme would succumb to the immortal evil spirit that was the Shadow Stealer. All the individuals I had rescued would be readily re-possessed, and the kingdom doomed.

Then I got a notion. My father, the senior Roan Quigley, survived. Apart from my gladness of the moment, I had always valued his advice. Maybe he would have some for me now. At least I could see him again.

I teleported north. At some other time I would have enjoyed the experience of exercising my phenomenal new abilities, but this was business. When I saw the army, I focused on my father's mind trace, then jumped to his presence.

He was just finishing a military meal, looking exactly as I remembered him. "Hello, son," he said laconically, as if this were routine.

"Hi, dad." Then I couldn't help myself: I hugged him. "Glad you're alive. I was a mite concerned for a while."

"I got shot, but I got over it. Didn't have time to say farewell."

"How you doing, dad?" This seemed pedestrian and stupid, but at the moment I couldn't come up with anything better.

"Doing well enough, considering, son. I didn't feel so good when your mother died, but now I got me a new gal, and she's some creature, let me tell you. She's away most of the time, on business, but makes it really count when she gets together with me. Her other form is a dragon."

My jaw almost banged my collar bone on the way down. "Fiera!"

"You know her? Small Realm."

"I know her," I agreed, glad I had spared the dragon. "As a matter of fact, I'm a dragon myself. You've heard of the Dragon King?"

"Oh, yeah. The one the foul princess came to kill, only it wasn't me."

"I'm going to marry that princess."

He looked at me. "Now I'm not one to mess with your preference, son, you know that. I never said a word when you married that bitch who alimonied you. But this time you'd be better off with a scorpion."

"I love her."

He shook his head. "She must be really special in bed."

"She's a virgin. I haven't touched her."

He grimaced at my folly. "She's pretty; I'll give you that. But she'll kill you, son. I'm in a position to know."

"She was possessed by a Shadow. I'll banish that."

"Can't be. The Shadows are our friends."

This was going nowhere, and my time was limited. "Dad, I'm going to give you a mind full, telepathically. You need to trust me."

"I always trusted you, son, 'cept for your judgment of women. Let me have it."

I let him have it. In an instant he knew what I did.

"Phew! I've been hoodwinked. How can I help you, son?" He was always one for quick assessments and realism, able to turn on a dime when necessary. I liked to think that I had inherited some of that.

"Tell me how to defeat the Shadow King, who is even now teasing me by letting me talk with you. He'll abolish us both when he tires of playing with his food. I need a workable strategy right now."

He considered. "I'm not much for telepathic battle strategies. All I can think of is Hannibal and the Romans."

"Hannibal?" I asked blankly.

"I guess they didn't have ancient history in your school. I didn't pay much attention to it myself. But what I vaguely remember is that Hannibal was the general of the army of Carthage, in one of the Punic wars. He was really good, and the Romans couldn't touch him. He even invaded Italy, with his elephants, and for fifteen years ravaged the countryside, and they couldn't stop him. He teased them something awful. Once when he was in the area where the Roman general lived, he made sure to ravage all the land except what belonged to the general, making it look as if he'd been paid off."

"Good joke on the Romans," I agreed. "But dad, is there a point to this history?"

"I'm getting there, son. The Romans finally got smart. They figured that if they couldn't get Hannibal in their own land, maybe they could bring him to bay in his homeland, where he couldn't sneak away. So they laid siege to Carthage, really making it hard for the city. And Hannibal had to come back to defend his home. And they were ready for him, once he couldn't avoid them. I think he didn't have time to get his full army back, so was weakened. They destroyed him. By making him play their game, instead of his game."

I considered that. "You're saying I might do better in Shadowland?"

"You always were a bright lad," he said approvingly.

I wasn't sure of that, but played along. "Do you happen to know where Shadowland is, dad?"

"I do happen to know, because I've seen the minions going there for refresher courses or whatever. There's a hidden access right over that mountain pass." He pointed to a nearby mountain range.

Well, any notion was better than none. "Thanks, dad," I said, and teleported to the pass. I materialized just shy of it, turned dragon form, and winged on across. Would this work?

There was a flicker, and suddenly I was in a realm of perpetual gloom. That figured; this was the home of the Shadows, so it was all shadow. Now what would mess them up so badly that the Shadow King would have to come back to stop it?

Readily answered: light. Enough to banish all shadows. So I inflated, then breathed out a sheet of flame sufficient to make the sun pale in comparison. There was dry tinder on the valley floor, and it burst into flame, enhancing the effect. And I heard or sensed a faint wailing, as of things getting wiped out by all that intolerable light. Too bad for them. I kept blow-torching, covering as much area as I could. This was fun, in its destructive way. Maybe like the fun the Shadow King had when toying with me.

And he was there before me. *What are you doing?*

"Isn't it obvious?" I replied sweetly, knowing it was my mind rather than my words that he heard. My dragon words weren't very clear anyway, muffled by smoke. "I'm making a bonfire. Do you have any marshmallows?"

No! he thought in mixed rage and pain. Then, beset by the discomfort of the moment, he did something stupid: he tried to attack me physically, attempting to smother me in his ambiance. He was playing my game.

I directed a stream of fire right through the heart of his invisible cloud. Oh, that hurt; I could feel his agony. I had caught him with a sucker punch. But I didn't rest on my laurels; I kept firing, burning up the very air around and through him.

That was hardly the end of it, but now I had seized the advantage, and I never let up. I kept going until there was nothing left of the king and Shadowland but ashes.

The Shadow King was gone; I could feel it. I had defeated him, thanks to my father's advice. The menace of the Shadow Stealers had dissipated.

———

It took a few days to organize the chaos, such as abolishing any remaining Shadows, but we were all glad to do it. Dad, and Fiera in woman form, attended the wedding. Then Princess Rose and I set off on our honeymoon. Where? In Lost Angels, of course, and Mouse House, and all the theme parks. She had never had an experience like this, by day or night, when we made love. Meanwhile, I knew that First Concubine Mave and Second Concubine Ellie were preparing the castle for our return, when I would do my duty by them. I expected to enjoy my sojourn there.

So what about the Dragon King? He wasn't much for incidental daytime activities. He receded into the depths of my being, there to wait quiescently until the next crisis, which I hoped would not be in my lifetime. With luck he wouldn't have to manifest again until the time of our grandchildren, if then.

Given a choice between the two worlds, I chose the Realm. Back on earth, I was still divorced and still in debt. Imagine the surprise of my ex-wife when discovered that a small fortune in gold—enough to pay 100 years of alimony—had been deposited into her bank account.

I might be the Dragon King…but I'm still a gumshoe at heart. Dragon King, P.I.

I like the ring of it.

The End

Also available from
Piers Anthony and J.R. Rain

Aladdin Relighted
The Aladdin Trilogy #1
Kindle * Kobo * Nook
Amazon UK * Apple * Smashwords
Paperback * Audio Book

New from Piers Anthony:

Board Stiff
A Xanth Novel
Kindle * Amazon UK * Paperback

New from J.R. Rain:

Zombie Patrol
Walking Plague Trilogy #1
Kindle * Kobo * Nook
Amazon UK * Apple * Smashwords
Paperback * Audio Book

ABOUT THE AUTHORS

Piers Anthony is one of the world's most prolific and popular authors. His fantasy Xanth novels have been read and loved by millions of readers around the world, and have been on the New York Times Best Seller list twenty-one times. Although Piers is mostly known for fantasy and science fiction, he has written several novels in other genres as well, including historical fiction, martial arts, and horror. Piers lives with his wife in a secluded woods hidden deep in Central Florida.

Please visit him at www.hipiers.com for a complete list of his fiction and non-fiction and to read his monthly newsletter.

J.R. Rain is an ex-private investigator who now writes full-time. He lives in a small house on a small island with his small dog, Sadie, who has more energy than Robin Williams.

Please visit him at www.jrrain.com.

11184574R00081

Printed in Great Britain
by Amazon.co.uk, Ltd.,
Marston Gate.